Coelacanth

/siləkænθ/

VOLUME 12 — 2023

Published by Newman University

COELACANTH

STAFF

Editor-In-Chief	Hadassah Umbarger
Prose Editor	Emily Maddux
Prose Editor	Austin Schwartz
Poetry Editor	Bethany Griffiths
Poetry Editor	Dylan Sykes
Art Editor	Eliana Gaytan
Art Editor	John Suffield
Faculty Advisor	Bryan D. Dietrich

ACKNOWLEDGEMENTS

Sister Madeleine Kisner
Jeanne Lobmeyer Cárdenas
Newman University
Newman University Theatre Department
Newman University Art Department
Eighth Day Books
Sonny Laracuente
John Jones

Newman University is a Catholic University named for John Henry Cardinal Newman and founded by the Adorers of the Blood of Christ for the purpose of empowering graduates to transform society. Newman University does not discriminate on the basis of sex, creed, handicap, national or ethnic origin. Accredited by The Higher Learning Commission, 230 South LaSalle St., Suite 7500, Chicago, IL 60604. Opinions and beliefs expressed in *Coelacanth* are exclusive to the journal.

Copyright © 2023, all rights reserved.

CONTENTS

POETRY

Mai-Nhanh Dao	Ballet	7
Thomas Elliott	On Christmas Morning	8
	Still You are the same.	9
Rachel Gerbick	(A) Human Nature	10
Tatyana Hill	flower fall.	11
	God's grotto.	13
	i saw icarus die today.	14
	siren's serenade.	15
Sofia Jarski	love letter from an earthworm	16
	simon's not embarrassed to be seen with you	18
	the Artist	20
	throne rooms and stab wounds	21
Elise LeMonnier	He who visits in flight:	23
	The Frustrations of Elusivity	24
	The Shape I Take	26
Jaden Lynn	Not A Sexed Up Lyric	27
Claire McCarty	Wounds that Bleed Ink	30
Anna McElhannon	Holy	32
	To Cast a Shadow	34
Barri McGougan	2955 McGougan Mill Pond Road	35
Naheda Nassan	6,800,000	38
	Grieving a Hypothetical Me	40
	To my father who will never reconcile with the country that raised him	41
Zackery Rodick	Routine	42

Samuel Schmidt	Divine Mirth	43
	Taraxacum	45
Austin Schwartz	Haikus	46
	The Night Death Found Joy	48
Kayla Shields	Drinking My Pain Away	50
	When I lift the Weight Off My Shoulders	51
Hope Strickbine	Autumn's Gift	52
	Common Xanadus	53
	Waves	54
Hadassah Umbarger	Eden	55
	Honey Sun	56
	Lantern	57
	Sacristan	58
Canaan Walker	Border State	59
	N49°21'59", W121°44'50"	60

ART & PHOTOGRAPHY

Julian Garcia	Cellular	62
	Dagenham Dream	63
	Mrs. Rabbit	64
	Screw Wave	65
Eliana Gaytan	Dragons	66
	Recreation of Raphael's Madonna of the Lilies	67
Alivia Nguyen	A Bench	68
	Coral	69
	Mother Drinking a Cup of Tea	70
Samuel Schmidt	The Father's Gaze	71

Taylor Peden	Landscape03c	72
	Abstract07	73
John Suffield	Dracula	74
	Rambo with a Beard	75
	Triton's Throne	76
Kirstin Richmeier	Jittery	77
Hadassah Umbarger	But if I had a pigeon, maybe	
	I'd name him Barnaby	78
	Thicc Goose	79

PROSE

Eli Apple	Enamorization	81
Dominic Jirak	Ash: The Harbinger	95
Ila Kumar	What He Wants	99
Claire McCarty	The Most Perfect	
	Birthday Surprise	104
Victoria Micha	(Un)Happy Birthday to Me	109
	Venus Fly Trap	114
Kaylee Patterson	The Face of Death	120
Rachel Patterson	Ill-Fated	127
Austin Schwartz	Lantern's Light	138

DRAMA

Cynthia Chen	Charlotte and Amelia	142
Emily Maddux	The Significance	
	of Being Stupid	158
Austin Schwartz	Chekhov	168
John Suffield	The Company	181

COELACANTH

POETRY

Mai-Nhanh Dao

BALLET

As they twirl faster,
We move slower

As they jump and leap,
We stay grounded and deep

Western ballet
is not the same
As Cambodian Ballet

No leotards
No pointed feet
No pink shoes

But there are

Flexed hands
Flexed feet
Arched back

Both tell stories
Stories to be told

Despite the difference,
There is resilience

Thomas Elliott

ON CHRISTMAS MORNING

It has been cold and dark
in this winter world,
and silence stifled song.

But now, the dawn breaks,
and, longing for warmth, we turn our heads
and raise them to the light.

But what we see confuses us:
not heavenly star or blinding glory,
but a brother, a son of man.

He steps over the horizon,
and alights on earth,
and suddenly the Dawn I didn't know I sought
greets me with voice like mine.

STILL YOU ARE THE SAME.

Ah! what months can do to a place!
Strip it of bloom and clothe it with gold,
and still You are the same.

And Lord, I wonder:
Am I the same, or have I too changed?
What am I stripped of, and clothed with what?
Yet still You are the same.

I come to speak myself to You,
poorly, as my poor tongue can,
but still in strokes of ink made gold
by grace, for though I am very small,
still You are the same.

Yes, I am changed, but not for naught,
for naught has not a place in Providence,
and truly it was Your hand
that stripped me of the past
and clothed me with the present,
while still You are the same.

What does this mean for me?
That if I knew Your depth of Love,
with haste I would forget my fear,
and though Your dark profundity
confounds my eagerly searching eyes,
I choose to dive in nonetheless,
for Love in ages past bears witness
that still You are the same.

Rachel Gerbick

(A) HUMAN NATURE

Looking at her, I found it somewhat difficult to believe that any part of her was meant to be extraordinary. Brown hair and brown eyes, average height if not slightly tall, average build. She always sat with a slight slouch, her feet facing in towards each other, her hands always touching, the slightest smile on her face and a pair of wide eyes. It seemed as if she was trying to live quietly when you looked at her. Trying to blend in with her surroundings, the people around her, the very earth on which she stood. But she wasn't quiet. Her emotions screamed from within her words, her face, the movement of her hands. I always felt as if a piece of me belonged to her, a prized possession that she gently cradled in her hands. There was no end to her. Her love of the world and its people, her desire to understand and connect, the wonder and the questions and the answers. I don't think there was ever a chance that life or death could have contained her.

Tatyana Hill

FLOWER FALL.

through the haze of june,
    we were side by side on your back porch, sun - beaten,
      & dirtied from the garden that you couldn't stop killing.
you wanted a paradise, your own eden,
    but you always overwatered it,
you always gave the things you love a little too much,
until you were left staring at what you had drowned,
& it was the dying daffodils that caused you to give up.
    the emissaries of new beginnings
    that brought you to a disappointing end —
      i watched the revelation before you even spoke it,
your eyes reflecting the emptiness of the sky
    as you spoke around a mouth full of honeydew,
      "i'm tired of myself. i'm tired of the world."
i smell the sweetness on your breath & almost turn reckless &
    kamikaze.
i imagine our fingers intertwined.
        i imagine myself brave when i kiss
          you & say, *let's go make another.*
i'll create a world in full bloom,
      & tell you i love you through the sky raining
        roses.
when the storm breaks, in its aftermath, i'll gather
    a bouquet of carnation - colored clouds, a gift
      for when we marry beneath the eye of the primrose
        moon,
    sailing away in our gowns of bougainvillea.
        we'll drink tea & feed each other wedding

cake,
find land & build ourselves a kingdom,
our declaration
woven in a flag of lilac & monkshood,
for all to know
of this first love, this beautiful floral
monsoon.

GOD'S GROTTO.
Inspired by the Ave Maria Grotto in Cullman, Alabama

this land
of little jerusalem
tucked away in stone,
    built wholly
      from the ordinary —
          marbles & shells & shards
          of broken plate, marbles &
          beads & the shine of jewelry
          catching in the midday sun.
            each of them glint
                among the blooming azaleas
                & the winding pathways,
                a reminder of how heaven
                in the corner of the south
                    was built by a single
monk,
                who now quietly exists as
a replica among the others,
    a rendition of the man that shoveled coal
    & used those same hands to construct holiness,
        standing as a testament of faith,
            that there is something
              divine in
            the human imagination.

I SAW ICARUS DIE TODAY.
Inspired by Brueghel's, "Landscape with the Fall of Icarus"

the first thing i heard was his laugh,
a tinkle of silver, bell chimes in the breeze,
light as the feather that
floated down
into my open palm.

i saw him.
a boy with wings,
a boy wearing bird skin,
rising higher
to the outstretched arms of apollo,
who made the mistake
of brushing his fingertips
against the skin
of his lover's back.

i heard his body
before i heard the screams of daedalus.

the world slows
and his eyes meet mine.

he grins
and lets himself
rest in the embrace
of the sea.

apollo weeps.
the world continues to turn.
i smile back.

SIREN'S SERENADE

do you hear the rise and fall of it?
    the echo of my heart
        that beats beneath the moontide?
my voice is for no one but you.
    you and the hungry thing nestled between
        my ribs, snapping bone in its teeth,
        this demand to stain the
        rhythm of the night red.
you know it too, the lack of difference
    between love and a killer's intent.
    which is to say
    they are both deliberate.
    which is to say
        i will love you
        as a shark loves blood,
        as a lightning strike loves flesh,
        and as a wave loves to drag down
        the weight
        of a dying body.

    i love you.
    i sing.

Sofia Jarski

LOVE LETTER FROM AN EARTHWORM

and if my little spur-of-the-heart, twitch-of-the-fingers,
taste-of-the-eternal stirs, sparks, inspires
any sort of effect on you, then if it were up to me,
i'd be the moon.

as if i ever could be her, that gorgeous thing, so patient in the sky.

she's filled from head to toe with that steady, pure glow only the sun gives.
she isn't mottled with craters like me.
isn't burned by dirt and debris like me.

they say there's water on the moon, rivers, but i know
there are entire waterfalls yet to be discovered,
pouring silvery tidal waves,
                        crashing, raging.
                                          powerful and endless.
the kind of ethereal water you'd live forever in
                                   if you dove headfirst.

she keeps the waterfalls hidden in the darker sides, eclipses of the night.
undoes all the knots that the speeding spaceships tie. she's beaming.
moon-beaming, letting the sun's light stray down to us
                             tiny, weeping children below.

how silly we must look to the stars, watching down on us.
we think them twinkling, but they're only giving tiny shakes of their heads.
in the infinite void of space, with the sun so close and undeniably bright,
the context rings so clear: earth is a tiny piece of a whole bigger picture.
from the context of where we're standing on this dirt, the heavens look far away.

but it's all about perspective.

it's all about remembering to look up every once and a while.

i'd love to be a star like you.
don't care if i'm counted with the billions,
don't care if i never make it onto anybody's telescope.
don't care if some boy names me after some girl for her birthday.

i wouldn't need to be a part of some intricate constellation.
i only have to be there in the sky among them, counted with the infinite.

that'd be enough for an earthworm like me.

SIMON'S NOT EMBARRASSED TO BE SEEN WITH YOU

the breath, the bite, the grip when thorns have teeth.
the way you conquer your skin as it bleeds.
the twitch, the spit, hot blood on your brow.
choking when you can't even stand, let alone stand it.
you know, you know, you're not supposed to buckle underneath
    the weight,
swallow mouthfuls of dirt, of salt, of sin, but you do.

you carry the weight of the world alone.

the jeering has faded so quietly that you're alone in this crowd
face-down in dreary shame. they'd mock you if they ever heard
    your name.
they wouldn't laugh if they'd ever felt the same.

the sweat, the sting of tears, the shivers, the lost golden years,
so faded they might've been dreams. not long ago we huddled
around a warm wooden table and broke bread, and
now you're never going to eat again.

the sunlight sweet, the firewood sharp, the bend before the
    break,
the break that comes with the SNAP –
dark tides turn so fast
you don't realize someone else has come to your aid until
you realize someone else stands over you.

they take it up, take it in. bear the load so you can drink
the air, the relief, the respite, the share of the burden
put on another shoulder that doesn't deserve it
and you'd die to the nails, humiliation, air stale, thorns deep,
if you didn't have such sweet relief
if someone hadn't taken up the burden for you first

THE ARTIST

the Earth's just a masterful of the Artist's hand.
all of creativity dwells in the heart of creation,
and creation tries its hardest to return the favor.

even the trees change their colors with their moods.
even the sun and moon know to take turns with lights and darks,
golds and blacks.
even a spider is born with the inherent desire to create, to spin,
to weave.
nobody tells it to – it just does.

why, if not out of some inherent necessity to create?

the Artist carves out the mountains;
with clay, He shapes their grandiose figures, their rise-and-fall
edges,
and they stand so tall people make cities out of them.
look at us trying to put together pretty words and lovely sounds
and splashes of colors, all from the same desire
to describe love and tell stories and create.

we're children finger-painting alongside their father's easel.
but the Artist glances over, smiles at what we've done,
the shoddy but honest way we imitate
unparalleled, magnificent creation

THRONE ROOMS AND STAB WOUNDS

enter center throne room with head held low
in silence never felt before
    electrifying tangible terrifying wonderful
drop your bloody sword
    fall to your knees
    that splint at their caps
every scar on your skin
    birthed from blade

could you ever be able to look up and see?

heart begins to beat again
you feel it come alive
    burning, bursting, swelling, singing
a pit in your chest
    deeper than your heart
    deepest beyond the wounds

soul still intact
    despite it all

did your soul survive the war?
    does it need repairing?

reality heightened
every color alight like you've never seen
breathable thickness in the atmosphere
bask in the serene
    the kind of peace you never felt on a battlefield
        only saw in dream
    fulfilling, enlightening, rewarding

this is it. this is all.
this is everything.
> *you live for this, you fought for this*
> *you'd die for this*

even just a moment
in the presence of the king

Elise LeMonnier

HE WHO VISITS IN FLIGHT:

From the grainy egg of quail, comes arcing a fear of recollection
Chanting in the covers, walloping my ears and fettering my mind
Is it unspeakable? Or unspeakably tender?
Either way, it's circuitous.
Its innumerable
I try one two and I try three
I wallow through anecdotal antidotes, I let them dribble, melt, and inflate
They stay unabridged and coiled around my left palm
"This is the bitterness of tender and the bitterness of sorrow"
    sang the Sparrow
He wafts towards me in the awkward hours of
My trudging down and down
"Is it time for our annulment?" I call prudishly.
"Have you come to collect or for collection?"
I sharpen. How else can one speak?

THE FRUSTRATIONS OF ELUSIVITY

Prudence, matched by recognition raised from the tomb and for the frock.
Will you tell me the time? Will you tell me of my heart? And why it aches for something inexplicable and unexplainable?
The mist coils, at most, a shadow in disguise as a whisper. Bluish and ruddy it bites and stings
Where are you going? Will you not tell me?
Arching from the cosmos to the faux foxes and the orchids croaking and moaning through the bleary night
I can't breathe, I can't stand this
Where are you going? Where have you gone and how can I follow
can I drink the sinew of your spine and can I count the notches of your breath that pass by my skin when
you lean too close, far too close for one so far away.
And you won't tell me, you won't tell me how Lazarus was raised or how the shrew was tamed.
I can't roam forever even if it becomes me.
 I'm just a reconstruction
Of light and dust and ash and yolk
Elusively I chase you with words I cannot define and fragments of remorse that will not contain you.
It's five to noon and no I can't tell you and no I don't know why.
The susurrus of Spring and the bleeding of July, bemoanings too hot and too long for this Elusivity
The sprigs are blanched — a great rotten work for one so limpid in segregation
Your coyness rustles like the doe in the underbrush, in the alpenglow
Will you tell me? Will you take the seeds of my heart and coax them into the night?

He was raised and tamed at ungodly hours, so early and so late
   you refused him
Think of my misery. Think of me miserably.
How could This breathe, a reconstruction of life

THE SHAPE I TAKE

My enjoyment is pressed flesh against paper, like poppies in the
    extended copy, poppies don't press well.
They lose their color and leach onto words
Fragmentation and exaltation, salted and choked by plumes
Would this bring me close to you, even if I'm colorless,
Even if I'm flat, I'm spoken.
Can I be spoken if flatness is a requirement
How can I speak without the curve of your throat or the length
    of your hands. You are the shape I take.

Jaden Lynn

NOT A SEXED UP LYRIC

She say *I'm sexy*, twirling around on them chicken legs–
tossing back her mane of hair like she a wild horse breaking out
    of the stable only to
prance around the arena. Watching trainers admire and applaud
while them other horses fiercely snort their envy.

I say *Lord Jesus, baby girl you in 4th grade! Why you need to be sexy?*
This girl of mine shoots me this coy look under her comb length
    lashes,
luminous blues so mischievous paired with her corkscrewed
    plush lips–
darkened skin and freckles stretching to accommodate that grin.

My grin. This girl of mine beautiful, and she know it too.
I know I'm sexy 'cause I am, challenging me with them sticks she
    call arms bowed on her narrow hips.
This bitty peanut gonna make me lose 30 years of composure.
Gonna make me beat all them boys that come sniffing after that
    sass, get bit…

then bum around 'till she coddles them like a mommy playing
    with dolls.
I want to say *girl you not old enough to be sexy, no way no how.*
But I ain't born yesterday.
I know these grown ass men stop to tell me 'bout her eyes, offer
    to get her ice cream.

Could see her burlesque dancing, scrawny self strapped in them
    black heeled boots
like she not momma's princess no more.
Could see her desperate to be loved and too free spirited she
    can't turn them dollars away. Pulling
tricks at them booming clubs to be appreciated.

Could see someone kidnapping my baby,
drugging her up and calling her sexy while they rip away her
    childhood.
Could see that bullet wound between her precious brows,
some trophy for some shit who thought he owned all that pretty,
    all that brave.

She done startle me when she say *you know I'm always gonna be sexy
    momma, I got your sexy*. This girl
squealing like she know she in trouble when I grab her and
sit back down with her on my porch rocker. But I ain't trying to
    be coming down with that
punishment. No ma'am, just want to hold my child 'fore she
    gone.

I say *get me that wax miss sexy*. She tittering when she does, and I
    braid her hair.
She say *I am sexy momma* quietly. Love this girl of mine's
    confidence. But I can
only offer a noncommittal murmur, meaning 'no' for me and
'maybe' for her.

How you supposed to protect your daughter when she
    headstrong?
    How you gonna tell her that there is no street, block,
        or city where sexy
            ever safe? Need her to be too young to
            understand just yet
                why momma be crying for her future
                as a woman.

Just keep rocking this part of my heart like this muggy morning is a forever memory.

Claire McCarty

WOUNDS THAT BLEED INK

The is pen mightier than the sword
for it is double-edged and stabs
me with every word its tips paint.
It is a dagger of pain that
promises to be my defense
to protect and free me
from the dungeon within,
yet while my soul's dying,
it's backstabbing and lying
and opening the wounds
once healed, but bleeding now anew.

It promises to help me escape
but as I run and run from that place,
that tower of fear, trying to flee
I realize it's pulling me
down the stairs of agony
and I fall deeper and deeper
into the crypts of despair.

From the bottom of my heart
from the depths of my soul
I look around to see a graveyard.
The tombs of mistakes, regrets and
doubts are neatly boxed there
and on their gravestones no
epitaphs only dry laughs and eerie smiles
that never die, their mockery

resounds for miles and miles
for though they are buried six feet under
they live inside and shake me like thunder.

My thoughts fly across the page
like a murder of crows they
are darker than the midnight sky
they circle round and round
like vultures do around carnage
their prey? My hope. I pray
they don't tear it to shreds for
it deserves a proper funeral,
since it will find no peace below
in the company of the ghosts that haunt me.
If birds of prey fly together,
so too thoughts of hope die together.

I search for a promise of gold
although I can clearly see its foil,
under the cloak of comfort is Torment,
she promises relief but bears agony
and massacres the last bit of peace I have in me
she's two faced and double sided yet I
release her and unsheath her fury
giving her reign over my mind again
and all with the single click of a pen.

Anna McElhannon

HOLY

It is holy
the air I breathe
dusty cardboard nativity
Above, a chorus chants
reaching into my chest

It is holy
The memory of
raised hands
celestial connections
In peaceful naivety
    thinking all knowledge
    is known by One

It was holy
when my father baptized me
in the waves, at the beach
He wasn't a preacher
I didn't care
My body rocked
in the frothing ocean
until I forgot
how dead men float

It was holy
the abandoned cathedral
at the art show in Winder
There were tattered bibles
in broken pews
Sun was shining through
the cracking yellow windows
In clouded vision I remember thinking
I wish I was good
at believing

TO CAST A SHADOW
After Anne Sexton

The moon is falling shut; I remember outer space holds
    shadows.

I can't remember why I'm here. Outside in
the warm night where the crying crickets and the humming pool
and the darkening moon are all that occupy my mind.
In another country people die.

At the observatory, I have to adjust the telescope. I watch
EV Pisces every night, but until I crank the lever
and aim the dome, I forget that I have a moving home.
I want to be at the observatory tonight.
In another country people die.

The moon is falling shut; it is massive. Some nights
when I close my door, sleep drapes itself over me. Then cracks
    of light settle,
and I can see- the earth, the sun, the moon. I can see our
    silhouette's reflection.
It is burning red.

I care for nothing; in another country people die.

Barri McGougan

2955 MCGOUGAN MILL POND ROAD

A speck on the map, Bethune, South Carolina has a radius of
 only a mile.
I visit twice a year, a place that is no longer my home, yet I
 feel

smothered, unable to escape everyone knowing my last name,
who my dad is or what I looked like the last time they saw me.

Winding down our dusty road, sparsely covered with red dirt
 and
chipped fragments of gravel, I travel back to the place I was
 raised.

A road with ruts so deep I feel almost as if I could fall into the
 earth, sink down
into this small-town lifestyle, a lifestyle I have outgrown.

Sometimes I miss the way it feels to drive down that road.
Each bump of the car when it dips down into a deep rut,

to come to an end and see our double wide with a wooden front
 porch,
a beautiful pond where I spent so much time as a child.

Cicadas chattering, a chorus of bullfrogs,
the distant crow of my grandmother's rooster.

I can hear yelling reverberating off the pale-yellow walls,
the same color they have been since before I was born.

Tall pine trees pass by the window, and they could be my father's
   Michelob bottles—
counting how many he has had, waiting until it's been one too
   many.

The thought of drinking throws me backward like the kick of a
   rifle and I am
throwing away baby dolls, or clothes we left lying on the floor.

My friends ask me, *Why won't you drink with us?*
It's not their fault that they can't understand

that sinking feeling of if I let myself do it, even just once,
I will become someone I am not.

I am my father's daughter—

The thought of alcohol, I can hear my parents arguing,
over money, drinking, God knows what else has pissed my dad
   off.

But I can also hear bursts of laughter, like bells chiming in the
   church steeple.
The past is gone, I only come here now during

weeklong breaks from school, visiting for holidays with family.
These memories make me question who I am, how I will treat
   my children.

All I can think about is that steering wheel in my hand and the bumps and grooves of that long, winding road, reminding me of how far I have come.

Naheda Nassan

6,800,000

like strays
wandering
through cities unknown
to them
and their children
taking what fits
in the knaps
on their backs
they are lost
not because
they don't know
their way
but because
they can't go back
abandoning all
they've known—is it abandonment if it's not a choice?
their child cries
for her friend
who lives across the street
"She doesn't live there anymore."
"We don't live there anymore."
she is too young
to understand
war and how
it lingers
like the smell
of smoke
from the fires

hanging
in the air and
staining your clothes

GRIEVING A HYPOTHETICAL ME

i am jealous
of this older version of me:
> *she's twenty*
> *was able to see*
> *her father's country*
> *before it became debris*

it's no longer free
strangled by tyranny—a leader who believes in silencing

TO MY FATHER WHO WILL NEVER RECONCILE WITH THE COUNTRY THAT RAISED HIM

to the lemon slushies
around the corner
for ten lira
and the Superman chips
baked into swirls
dipped in The Laughing Cow

to the cat
that chased the mouse
for my brother and I
and the orange kitten
we found behind the mosque
and kept

to the shop owner
selling notebooks with gems
i begged dad for
and the uncle
who traced my palms
while i sat in his lap

to the cousin
twisting tissues
tickling my nose
and to Wageeh
and Waseem
and Mazen
whom i lost
before i could hold

peace be with you.

Zackery Rodick

ROUTINE

All I do now is hurt,
And I tell myself:

                                      I'm doing it because
                                                    Of you.
                                      I'm doing it for you.
                             I'll do it if you want me to.
                        I'll do it since you want me to.

I'm doing it for myself.
I'm doing it because
Of the way I am,
And always have been,
And always will be.
                    I would have done it
                             Regardless of your presence.

That hurts.

Samuel Schmidt

DIVINE MIRTH

How can You possibly request
    My feet not touch the ground?
For human nature is fallen,
    Our tendency is down.

Rising is not within my soul,
    My heart is made of earth,
And so I cannot obey these,
    Your statutes must be Mirth.

The angels float, so command them
    To not swear oaths nor lie,
Nor divorce spouse, nor be angry
    Or love their enemies.

But I'm human, I cannot bear
    The weight; I surrender.
In Wisdom's plea, I'm bound for hell
    I cannot rise to her

Yet how I hear a cry of man;
    "Father, Forgive!" resounds.
His hands and feet nailed to a tree
    He's lifted off the ground

I was correct, its Divine Mirth
    That asks me to obey,
For nails within the hands of God
    Reveal the only Way.

TARAXACUM

So calm it sits, with yellow blossom bright
    Within the crack of concrete gray,
Adding to the dull stone a welcome life,
    Unfettered by what some may say.

For some call it a weed, and so it is
    Only to they who call it that.
Of the reality, their labels miss,
    But it's secure, it will come back.

It is the greatest flower of them all,
    Resilience it's mighty charm,
Or transformation to dust that enthralls;
    A fitting gift to give to mom.

But perhaps to be taken up in awe
    One must be small.

Austin Schwartz

HAIKUS

Zebras have the stripes.
The lions do not, oh well!
Jungle knows its king.
***
The guitar strings hum
A love letter unwritten.
The bard sleeps alone.
***
My heart's pulse ceases,
My life wrenched from my soul.
Don't trust computers.
***
A wind knocks my door.
I let the breeze in my home.
Now there's cold in warmth.
***
A dark protector,
Hidden in the shadowed night.
The black sky: a hero's light
***
An undead monster
Wants to stop its pain, live free.
Villain it must be.

***

The blue water quakes
Bottomless is the blue sea
"unknown" rolls the sand

***

Late to class again
The pretty girl wants to date
Spidey sense, "why now?"

THE NIGHT DEATH FOUND JOY

There was no scream when her car slid across the ice.
Considering the circumstances her expression was quite plain.
Some might say it was what she wanted; no regrets or "what if's."
Her heart was settled and shortly after the car broke through.
As the water started pouring in, her eyelids never rose.
In those last moments, maybe, there was regret, the end did not bring her joy.

Throughout life, few things brought her joy.
Her mother always stared at her with those dead pan eyes.
She would sigh and steadily drag the spoon through her soup as the ferryman rows.
For a while she would try little tricks as her mom once did for her, "here comes the plane."
But, mom just got mad and threw
The spoon for no good reason she could think of.

Her brother, on the other hand was full of imagination. If
We play pirates can I play Captain Joyce?
She'd always walk away before his childish prodding was through.
Then he'd let out a few, "Aye-Aye's!"
Run into the living room where he was play'in
And set the chairs up into two rows.

"Come play with me Rose!"
Her heart began to beat faster as if
She were sinking. She was, and her soul was about to leave this plane.
She had known joy. Her brother was that joy.
Suddenly, she opened her eyes.

Reminding herself not to breath, she grabbed the seatbelt at the clip, and threw.

Rose wasn't through, her brother wasn't through, not even her mother was through.
Cutting her ankle across the glass, she let out a scream. Her last bubbles of air rose
Toward the surface. Tauntingly they didn't even pop, only bounced off the ice.
Now her brother, Matty, was all she could think of
The seafaring fun they could have together in his pirate loving joy.
"Damnit!" She'd give anything to be out of this water laying out in a grassy plain.

She was now grimacing, her eyebrows furrowed. Her expression was far from plain.
Her knuckles bled red before her pounding on the ice was through.
That night, when the water stilled, death found joy.
Rose's body sunk down to where Charon rows.
The last thought she had was of
Matty's "aye-ayes!"

The funeral was two weeks later.
Matty, looked through the tears in his eyes at his sister and laid a rose on her chest. Regretfully, he
thought, "If mom died in that plane crash, you'd still be here. I'd still have my joy."

Kayla Shields

DRINKING MY PAIN AWAY

    We clink our glasses, drinking till dawn.
I collapse my breath to the breeze beneath your
bow, and beam my arrow toward your narrowed love.
The ring of red flames encapsulates the point. I Ignite
the flare that coresses your berried lips. As I draw the
bow at your beloved heart, the blood melts
to the bottom of the glass, you
only sipping,
until
the
last
bit
is too bitter to take anymore.

WHEN I LIFT THE WEIGHT OFF MY SHOULDERS

An hourglass, its sand shifts
from one side to another.
Grits of brown and beige
make a barren desert.
I trudge through the sand
to the point where I can't breathe.
Feet treading sand.
That's the issue with time,
there isn't enough of it.
At this point I'm falling, far below,
to the deepest part of the glass,
where I will no longer be found.
Where my light will die slowly.
The cavity of my body is swallowed
by sand and heat.
And in that tiny moment,
there is silence and peace.
Until the hourglass is reset.
And then once again,
I'm drowning.

Hope Strickbine

AUTUMN'S GIFT

The rising sun both lights and robs the earth
Of its morning's diamonds and pearls
Revealing the splendor as it takes it away

The silent sentinels' cloaks crackle
Crimson, ruby, and gilded bits of color that float through the air,
Drawing my eye to the riches all around
As the wind removes the well-earned wealth of the sentinels

Removing their gilded cloaks so they may have their season's rest
And aiding them in their dance as the sun turns them into a
    shifting stained glass
More beautiful than that of any cathedral

COMMON XANADUS

Zeniths abound
Years come and go
Xanadus more often come around
Weather changes with the seasons, we all know
Vistas are worth treasuring

Ultimate beauty always worth the journey
Treasure found in the most common places
Staying or straying our sight's often blurry
Recognizing worth takes seeing graces
Quiet places, often most alluring

Passing time reveals new splendor
Observation takes much skill
Never presume the value rendered
Magic and wonder bestill
Look close to find the worth enduring

Keeping hold of memories
Joyous or tender, but treasured
Images seen through the centuries
Help to heal with time deferred
Guide through trials immuring

Finding the place we belong needs time
Every day, a chance to apprehend the mist
Daring to believe, in meantime
Common xanadus exist
But sometimes need un-obscuring

Awesome wonders forever enduring

WAVES

Rolling white foam and breathless blue
Thinning and bunching in rapid currents
Currents that bend and sway
Creating waves below
Gold and green; spring and pine
Scattered and treasured

Space and time, mass and energy, ebb and flow
Remote and ticking, astronomical currents
Currents that pull and flow
Creating the waves below
Silver and marine; cold and breathless
Mirrored

Love and hate, compassion and greed, strength and feebleness
Currents that drive and move the waves below
Oblivious and monotonous
Too afraid to leave

The currents they have been stuck in
Since the beginning of time

Hadassah Umbarger

EDEN

No, my dear.
If you want to write poetry
please abstain from the bulbous moon
hanging in the sky like forgotten fruit,
or the sky-blue ocean or ocean-blue sky
and your heart as restless as the dancing tide—
tell me about the dog, shitting on your lawn.

HONEY SUN

I can't write poetry, because I'm happy.
It's only when I'm in pain that it works,
if I'm going to bleed, I'll bleed beauty.
But today I saw the honey sun on the carpet,
and I said one day maybe I'll have my own house
with my own sun
and, you know, I entirely believed it possible?

LANTERN

You mean to tell me that there are people
who step outside at night and don't even
think about looking at the moon?
She was late and yellow last night and I wanted
to cry.

The nights where she's blindingly white
and casts shadows are my favorite.
She doesn't need much from me,
simply lets me stare and smile
while she tells me about the things she's seen—
queens killing lovers
poets going mad
wild dances in forests
whispered oaths.

SACRISTAN

Today I walked into the sacristy
to find the crucifix broken.
His corpse lay pieced on the windowsill.

His face looked up at me calmly, limbless
as if being completely shattered
was normal, to be expected
from a people who had forgotten.

Canaan Walker

BORDER STATE

the tail end of summer
brings a familiar chill to the air
trees once engulfed in green foliage
transition to sapphire
red,
orange,
and yellow flames
that spark forests in the fall
and cover the ground with embers
as the temperature drops
the incoming season promises
an endless slew of snow,
with time for a final road trip north
before our tiny town is buried in white
Dad packs the flatbed, Mom packs the snacks
my sister and I wait in the backseat
sharing headphones over the DVD player
buzzing with the Full House box set on repeat
the truck shakes as the tailgate closes
"six hours to Niagara Falls!"
my dad shouts, taking his place at the steering wheel
as I watch a golden leaf hit the ground from the window

N49°21'59", W121°44'50"

summers in British Columbia
meant riding my uncle's jet boat
to and from town—
the only way to reach
serene comfort of cached cabin
resting on the bottom
of pine tree cloaked mountains
once a year, we'd endure
washing our clothes
in a Canadian Tire bucket
bubbling with liquid detergent
and lake water that my dad deemed
cleaner than crystal,
managing nights with no electricity
unless it was an emergency
like watching a VHS from the collection

ART & PHOTOGRAPHY

Cellular

Julian Garcia

Dagenham Dream

Julian Garcia

Mrs. Rabbit

Julian Garcia

Screw Wave

Julian Garcia

Dragons

Eliana
Gaytan

Recreation of Raphael's Madonna of the Lilies

Eliana Gaytan

A Bench

Alivia Nguyen

Coral

Alivia
Nguyen

Mother Drinking a Cup of Tea

Alivia Nguyen

The Father's Gaze

Samuel Schmidt

Landscape03c

Taylor
Peden

Abstract07

Taylor
Peden

Dracula

John Suffield

Rambo with a Beard

John
Suffield

Triton's Throne

John Suffield
and
Hadassah Umbarger

Jittery

Kirstin Richmeier

But if I had a pigeon, maybe I'd name him Barnaby

Hadassah Umbarger

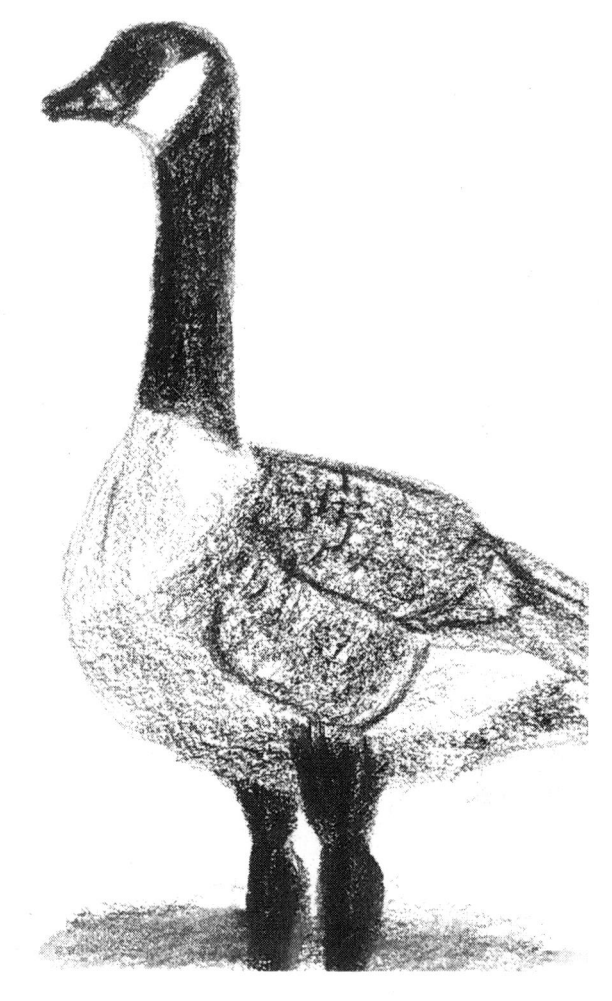

Thicc Goose

Hadassah Umbarger

PROSE

Eli Apple

ENAMORIZATION

    Cameron looks at the apartment and leans against the metal door behind him, its cool press against his back as he pushes it back into place, his hands splayed out against the wooden wall. His fingers meet the grooves in the wood and dig in.
    It's not dark inside, as he had anticipated. Instead, the apartment is lit up in shades of purple, green, and red from the neon signs hanging along the walls. An "OPEN" sign flashes on the center of the wall directly across from him, each letter flickering on one at a time. "O," then "OP," then "OPE," then "OPEN," the sign briefly reads for a second at a time before the cycle is repeated. He can see a hallway glowing to his right that stretches out of his sight, the sole door leading away from the living room area he now stands in.
    He continues his scan of the room, his eyes coming to rest for a moment at a poster to his left, bathed in green light from a sign in the shape of a cannabis leaf right above it. It's one of those National Geographic posters that kids can tear out of their magazines and hang in their rooms. *Did you know?* it reads, *Dolphins have two stomachs!* A dolphin splashes along the middle of the poster, its body rising out of the water as it looks right at the viewer. Its teeth gleam in the picture, stretched up in such a way that the dolphin almost looks as if it's smiling for the camera.
    Cameron already knew this fact. It was one of those random things that Josie had picked up from her time as a marine biologist, an interesting piece of knowledge that she had passed on to Cameron once she signed on as his advisor for his PhD program. *One stomach for storing the food, the other for digestion,* he thinks now, her voice echoing in his head. Looking at the neon

signs, the poster, the lighted hallway sends a rush of goosebumps down Cameron's arms, and he arches his back to try and shake the sensation that's building in the pit of his stomach. Something's not right in this apartment. He shouldn't be here—already his hand is coming back up to reach for the handle, to take him back out into the hall. He's seen enough. But it's the smell that stops him, that freezes his hand in the middle of turning the handle. The aroma invades the room, an army of soldiers armed with pungent wintergreen guns and grape swords waging war against his nose. He had been able to smell it down from the first floor of the complex—it had been the smell, after all, that had led him up here and prodded him to turn the unlocked door handle and investigate—though now that he's inside the room, the smell becomes almost unbearable. He can barely move, he's so overwhelmed by it.

It's what I thought it was, though, Cameron thinks as he brings the collar of his leather jacket to press up against his nose, trying to muffle the stinging that rings inside his nostrils. A year ago, he had been working in the lab with Josie—they were supposed to be working on his dissertation, but instead of researching and evaluating the factors that allow for maximum production of tetrahydrocannabinolic acid synthase and its concomitant effects on THC levels in marijuana plants, the two of them aimlessly combined alcohols and acids as he created various esters, when he had felt the same stinging in his nose that he did now. He had rushed to the sink, the cool glass of the beaker pressing against his hands as he poured the mixture out and hoped that the scurrying of water down the drain would take the smell with it. But it stayed in the room, and as he coughed he looked up and saw Josie standing, arms akimbo and a small frown on her face as she watched him.

"It's butyl salicylate," she said, reaching one hand to pull out the esterification chart she had given him, which Cameron had lost under a stack of beakers and graduated cylinders. Her finger came to rest upon a laminated square at the intersection of *butyl* and *salicylic acid*. Over the image of a wintergreen leaf, the word STRONG was written in all capital letters.

"You knew that was going to happen?" Cameron asked, though as soon as Josie had pulled out the chart he had known the answer.

Josie stared at him for another second, tucking a strand of black hair behind her ear before setting it on his shoulder as she said, "Be more careful with what you're mixing." In her eyes, the words *Of course I knew* were written. Looking at her, Cameron had imagined pressing his mouth to hers, beakers shattering around their feet as he swept everything off the lab table and set her on it, his hands becoming lost as they searched for stars in the space of her hair. She was at the table over from him; he could reach her in two large steps if he wanted to. But he had held himself back. That time.

Head still adjusting to the smell, he finally begins to process his sense of sound, and he hears a series of sounds ring out against the silence of the apartment complex in rapid succession.

The first sound he hears is voices, talking low in the hall to his right. His hand, jolted once again into action, grasps the handle, and as he begins to turn it, he hears another, this time coming from his pocket. As he stands there, the ping of his phone reverberates through the apartment.

He freezes, his hand loosening on the handle as he reaches for his phone. He only has time to read the name *Josephine* across his screen—Josie thought it would be better to maintain a semblance of formality on his phone, at least in name, in case someone else happened to see his messages—before he hears the thud of boots sounding from the hall. Cameron doesn't even have the time to put his phone away before a head pokes out from behind the edge of the wall.

Cameron jumps back so fast that he knocks his head against the frame of the door. He can only see the person's head, but a mask covers their face, its features distorted in mock fright. A bright blue hood reaches up, covering the rest of their head.

The summer after his first year at undergrad, in the days when he told himself that he wanted to someday be a nurse, Cameron had interned at a hospital. As he started to work, his idea had been shattered after an uncountable amount of blood draws and physicals, the endless exams dripping from one day to the next. Eve, the main nurse he had been assigned to shadow, had been afflicted in childhood with some rare case of labyrinthitis that had never gone away and still proved unable to be cured, and so he had spent the majority of that summer trailing behind her, reordering the carts that she occasionally bumped into when she lost her balance and counting down the days until he could return to studying. But the one image that stayed with him more than any other from that time at the hospital was born on the day Eve showed him how to conduct an echocardiogram. He had stood there, his eyes rapt as he watched the incessant beating of a nameless patient's heart in black-and-white on the screen before him. As hard as he tried to envision a heart, however, he could only see a face on the screen, two large eyes and a hole for a mouth, twisted and disfigured in a perpetual scream. Cameron had thought that the heart didn't look unlike the man from that Munch painting. Shortly after that, he had his first glimpse of death when he witnessed an autopsy while shadowing at the hospital morgue. The person's face had been turned away from him, and as he stood there Cameron had imagined their face looking like the face he had seen on that echo, twisted up in death. The facial distortion, the screaming, was now, in Cameron's mind, something that happened to everyone after they died.

And now, his back against the wall, a thin throbbing beginning in his head, Cameron looks into the macabre eyes of a mask that bears an exact resemblance to the face he had seen on the echo. He freezes, his legs locked in place, when the figure speaks, emerging from behind the wall and coming towards him.

He's still frozen in place when the masked figure approaches him, its grotesque mouth shaking as the figure behind it begins speaking. "You're here early!" she says, her cheery voice at odds with the mask covering her face. She comes up to him and takes his hand. For a long moment, she only stares at him, silent, the black eyes of the mask threatening to engulf Cameron's soul with every passing second. Except for the fact that no part of her skin is left exposed, she wears a nondescript outfit. Blue jeans are tucked into combat boots, and the arms of her royal blue hoodie end beneath a pair of thin surgical gloves. Her touch sends Cameron pressing further back into the door, and she laughs at his hesitation, standing up on her tiptoes to ruffle the golden curls of his hair. "Guess what they sent us tonight," she calls out to whoever lies beyond the hallway, "it's a blond beauty, everyone!"

Cameron hears a burst of laughing applause flare up from within that hallway, when the girl tightens her grip on his hand and leads him down into it. Her grip is iron, her pace implacable as she leads him down the passageway with the force of a ship breaking through arctic floes of ice. Still too stunned to resist, Cameron can only be towed along in her wake.

"What—" Cameron tries to say, but she's already speaking, silencing him before he can say anything else.

"Don't say anything," she says to him. "It all goes easier that way." There's a quick moment of silence, and then she adds, "Plus, if you talk we'll have to put duct tape over your mouth."

Cameron has no idea what to make of this; his mind has been taken doubly captive by confusion over what is happening and fear over it, above all fear of the screaming mask with those expressionless eyes.

I just need to talk to Josie, he thinks to himself. *She'll know what to do.* He can already imagine himself laughing about this with Josie at some point in the future, lips turned up in a thin smile at him as he recounted the story to her. And at the end, when he'd ask *Would you know what to do, if you were in that situation?* she would only lay her hand on his shoulder, her eyes smiling in a way that suggests she's thinking *Of course I'd know.*

Though, as far as the duties of faculty advisors go, Cameron thinks this—whatever this is—is a little bit above Josie's pay grade. She's supposed to be helping him with his dissertation—and she is, though the two of them are working on far more.

Where is Josie, anyway? She's the only reason he's here right now, as this strange girl leads him past a first door, a second, and then a third. He meets Josie at this apartment complex every Saturday at nine at night, and they're on a rigid schedule. Cameron brings the two yellow, almost comical hazmat suits that he keeps in his apartment, and Josie brings the lab equipment. Cameron is there before her every week, without fail, already dressed in his hazmat suit when she arrives, carrying a bag laden with chemicals into the first floor apartment that they've commandeered for their business. While she unpacks the bag's contents, he runs out to the car to carry in their portable fume hood.

Each session is the exact same, more reliable even than the scientific facts that Cameron has dedicated his life to studying. They begin with Josie giving Cameron his share of the money that they've earned over the past week. He counts the money and then pockets it wordlessly, and then the two of them put on the hazmat suits, their practiced movements awkward yet precise under the fluoropolymer suits, and begin to work.

The actual process of manufacturing LSD, Cameron has learned, is quite simple. He supposes that, if they were different people, procuring the necessary compounds would prove to be a challenge, but Josie has everything in her research lab, so all they have to do is spend time mixing chemicals under the fume hood, isomerizing and purifying what begins as lysergic acid and ends as pure LSD. The hardest part, in his opinion, is converting the solution into a distributable form. They don't use blotter acid, but rather turn the solution into microdots of LSD, a process that Cameron still has not learned to master even after almost a year of practice. The only thing left to do after that was sell it, though it was far too risky for either of them to do that themselves. They part ways every Saturday, and Josie meets with another man, where she exchanges their supply of LSD in exchange for cash—though how she met him, Cameron has no idea.

About six months after they started their business, they began to add one more task to their routine. One Saturday, after they had disposed of their chemical waste and started taking off their hazmat suits, Cameron had looked over at Josie, at the sheen of sweat resting on her brown skin and the thin strand of hair that had fallen across her forehead. The adrenaline high of their business still running in a frenzy through his veins, Cameron had reached over and brushed that stray lock of hair behind her ear. She had looked up at him, her lips parted, and before he could think Cameron leaned over and pressed a kiss against her lips. He had jolted back just as fast, an apology already forming at his lips about how, for that second, he had forgotten that she was married, that she was his dissertation advisor, and for a second she hadn't been Josephine to him but just Josie. But before he could say anything, sitting there and opening and closing his mouth as he searched for the right words, Josie had leaned back over and then she was kissing him, and he pressed his starving mouth against hers and they fell back, the discarded hazmat suits cushioning their bodies as they pressed against the floor. Now, almost mechanically, they moved towards each other every week as soon as their hazmat suits were off, an illicit union born in the midst of their illicit business. He lay on the floor, the chill of the suits beneath him and Josie on top of him, and thought that he had never felt more alive.

His repeated trips to the apartment complex were born as a result of his desire to quantify the artistic, to understand that which could never have a specific solution. When he thought of her, he thought as much of the sensation of the hazmat suits, of the flopping inward of his lungs that he felt every time he was near her. More than anything, he sought to understand his own feelings, to figure out what it was about Josie that made him feel as though she could act as a substitute for all of those resources necessary for his survival.

He was obsessed with her. Kyle was in the same PhD program as him, and Cameron's thoughts of Josie dominated their conversations. Cameron kept him updated on everything, despite Kyle's halfhearted protests. The first time he had had sex with Josie, Cameron had called Kyle after, before his car had left the parking lot, and told him everything.

"Bro, come on, there's no way," Kyle had said. "You can't just say this without giving me some sort of proof."

Life had continued in this way. But this week, she had never shown. Cameron sat on the floor of that empty apartment for thirty minutes, a yellow smear against the wall in his bright hazmat suit, waiting for her to arrive as though he were waiting to breathe, but there was nothing. He hadn't wanted to go straight home, having driven out to this complex, an hour's drive away and two cities over from the one in which he lived, so when he had walked out of their apartment and caught a whiff of that unmistakable butyl salicylate, curiosity had encouraged him to explore. The thought that some other group of people, their faces hidden behind masks of death as they performed unknown illicit acts, would also have chosen this same complex as their base of operations had never crossed Cameron's mind.

He needs to check his phone, to see the text that Josie sent him and tell her to help him, *now*. But already they've reached the end of the hallway and the masked girl in front of him is pushing open the cracked door, leading him into the room with the voices.

Again, this room is lit by neon signs scattered around the room. He sees more of the cannabis-shaped signs, as well as a red one that reads "IT WAS ALL A DREAM" in flowing, cursive script. This time, however, three figures stand scattered throughout the room, each of them masked and wearing the same nondescript blue hoodie and jeans as the girl in front of him, who lets go of his hand now that they're in the room. In the center of the room, there's a plastic inflatable pool, filled almost to the brim with a cloudy, translucent liquid. Its circular border is fashioned in the style of a watermelon, with one green layer and another red one peppered with mock black seeds.

"You're tonight's volunteer?" one of the masked figures calls out, though he continues before Cameron has a chance to speak. "Good. You should already know a little bit about what we're doing from the ad, but just as a precaution, we need to implement some safety measures," he says, drawing out each syllable of the last two words and drawing a roll of duct tape out from the pocket of his hoodie.

"But—" Cameron starts.

"Shhhh. Don't worry, this is just for your own protection," he says, his voice gentle as his hands press down a thick strip of tape across Cameron's mouth. He does a terrible job of it, though, and a corner of the tape sticks up and agitates the side of his cheek. Cameron kicks out, but two other figures rush to his sides and hold down his arms at his sides, ignoring the muffled sounds of Cameron's yells against the tape. Cameron starts to move his hand up, to knock these figures away from him, but at that moment he feels a fourth figure press an arm against him from behind, taking his arms and tying them behind his back, then tying his legs together. He's pushed down into a wooden chair, unable to move.

"Great," the lead figure—the one that slapped the tape over Cameron's face—says, clasping his hands together over his chest. "Now that that's settled, let's get you filled in on what's about to happen." He pauses as if for dramatic effect, waiting to see how Cameron will react, but he only raises his head to knock a stray blond curl away from his eye, still yelling against the tape. In the silence, Cameron looks around, trying to differentiate the masked figures around him, hoping to make eye contact with one and convince them that they have the wrong person. The Leader of the five stands in front of him, his tall, stocky frame impossible to miss. To his left, two girls—the one that had led him into the room and the one that had tied his hands and legs—stand, whispering to each other.

"It's five minutes, right? In and out," one of the girls is saying to the other.

"Yeah, I think so."

The final figure has retreated to the back of the room and stands in a rivulet of darkness, their head cocked in interest as they stare in his direction.

"As you should already know from our ad," the Leader continues, drawing Cameron's attention, each word pronounced with practiced precision, "we're currently conducting trials of a new drug that we're hoping to get out onto the market soon, and we need a few participants on which to try it out. That's what you're here for." Cameron's eyes widen, his thoughts flipping between two different matters in rapid motion: the first, *Oh my god I didn't sign up for this they've got the wrong guy*; the second, *Wow, two separate groups making drugs in this one complex. What are the odds?* He begins to protest against the tape, hoping the Leader will understand that he is not the volunteer that they think he is. But his shouts are muffled by the tape covering his mouth, and he can't move without flopping out of the chair and splaying out onto the floor.

Oblivious to his weak attempts at protests, the Leader continues his speech. "Here's the specifics. Our preliminary name for this drug is Clonoxo, and the idea behind it is that you don't take this drug, this drug takes you." He pauses again, waving out his arms as if to say *Cool, right?* "This pool you see behind me contains pure, unadulterated Clonoxo. We're going to lift you up and sit you back down in the pool, and then you're going to sit there. There's a brief period near the start where we have to submerge your head for about ten seconds, just to make sure the drug takes full effect, and then all you have to do is sit there. You'll be there for about five minutes while we monitor any physical effects the drug seems to be having on your body, and then we'll keep you here for a few hours just to make sure any side effects of the drug have worn off before you go.

"Oh," he adds, raising a finger. "About the *safety measures*," he says, once again lengthening every syllable of the two words. "Since we're still tweaking the drug, there's a chance that it could provoke certain unexpected side effects in your body. Nothing serious, though," he says, this time catching the fright in Cameron's eyes as they widen again. "Maybe just some unwanted fasciculations or something like that. You ready?"

No, Cameron thinks, his body already spasming with fear. His eyes widen and he protests to the four masked figures in front of him, his screams just barely leaking out from the loose edge of the tape against his mouth. He looks into the masked eyes of the Leader and thinks of that dolphin, wishing he had two stomachs. The butyl salicylate continues its assault on his nostrils, and he realizes that the source of the smell is the pool in front of him. Without waiting for his answer, the four figures surround him, each of them circling him while at the same time nearing him, and everywhere he looks he sees the frenzied beating of hearts screaming out in agony as they pick him up and begin to make their way toward the pool. Before he can even sound out a cry of protest, four pairs of hands lift him up, still sitting in the chair. They lead him over to the pool and, heedless of the screams coming from his tape-covered mouth, they unceremoniously tilt the chair and drop Cameron into the chest-deep liquid.

For a brief moment, he feels nothing, and he lets out a sigh of relief. *This is going to be okay*, he thinks to himself. He *knows* drugs: he's studying marijuana and making LSD, and even though he may not take drugs himself, he knows enough that a person can survive brief trysts with them. He may start having withdrawals tomorrow, but those will pass. And then: *Formication*.

Individual droplets of liquid crawl over his body as ants do a pillar of honey, their slimy trails leaving behind slick burn marks all over Cameron's exposed face and arms. Under the surface of the liquid, he begins to feel droplets burrowing their way under his skin, crawling around through his veins as he sits there, unable to move at all. As he begins to scream, he looks up and sees the four masks of the figures looking down on him, and then four pairs of arms reach down and shove his head underneath the surface.

What had been a colony of ants becomes a torrent of lions carving away at his skin, invading every open orifice. He feels his body jerking and convulsing, his legs kicking out into the open air. His face is finally lifted up from under the liquid, the tape having come free from his mouth, and a waterfall of Clonoxo pours out from Cameron's mouth and nose. He feels it still running through his veins as it courses through his body, replacing his blood and his air until he is nothing more than Clonoxo. It feels like his heart is dissolving.

The endless torrent continues to pour from his open mouth as he looks around at the room, his arms spasming, flopping against the sides of the inflatable pool. And in that final moment of his life, Cameron looks around and finds himself able to see through things, to glimpse beyond the curtain of time and space and under the death of these masked figures. He feels, with a clarity that startles him, fear floods his insides, as if his lungs are flipping over upon themselves. A fear that, impossibly, overpowers the burning sensation that's overtaken his entire body, and he thinks that this is the same emotion that he feels when he is with Josie. He looks over to the one figure that's been silent the entire time, staring at him with their arms akimbo, and his back goes limp, his head coming to rest against the watermelon edge of the inflatable pool.

The four remaining figures in the apartment stand over the pool, staring down at Cameron's corpse.

The woman that first led Cameron into the room is the first to take off her mask. Her hands shake so badly that she drops it, clattering to the floor as she sinks to her knees and places her head in her hands. "What *was* that?" she asks, looking up at the others. "What have we *done?*" Her voice cracks and splinters at the end, and she returns her face to her hands with a loud sob.

The Leader and the other woman remove their masks and hurry over to her side. The Leader—a middle-aged man with hair just beginning to gray—puts his arm around her. "Shh shh shh, hush now, it's going to be okay," he says to her. He looks around at the group, and his practicality is clear from the steel in his eyes. "We're going to get out of this," he says to no one in particular.

The first woman looks up at him. A tear stain runs down the side of her face and curves off of her right cheek. "How can you say that?" she says. "We just *killed* an innocent man, and all you can think is how *we're* going to make it out of this unscathed?"

The second woman voices her agreement. "Yeah, what did you even *put* in there?" she asks, a stray lock of her hair falling in front of her face. She pushes it back and continues. "Clonoxo's never done anything like this before. Nothing even close."

As the three figures continue talking, the fourth—the one who has remained silent the entire time—stays close to the pool, looking down at Cameron's mouth, twisted open in a scream in his death. She thinks that Cameron's face looks like her own mask.

Silently observing the scene, the last figure unpockets her phone, open to a message thread. The contact's name reads Kyle. The most recent message is from a week ago, but she still hasn't responded to it. It's a video, under which reads *He just sent me this. I thought you should know.* She doesn't play the video. She's already watched it enough times to know what she would find. She knows that if she hit the play button, she would see herself, filmed from behind, as Cameron pushes into her, and the tinny sounds of her moans would echo out into the dim room.

She closes that thread, then opens another one. The contact's name is *Cameron.* Her most recent message was sent to him not even a half hour ago, but he'll never read it. She'd sent him the same video that he'd first sent to Kyle, and under that, she'd written the same words she had told him time and again in her research lab: *Be more careful with what you're mixing.* She drafts a third message, and looks back up at Cameron without sending it.

    She cocks her head down at him, wordlessly examining the grotesque twists of his face, the burn marks that stretch across his exposed body and that disappear under the surface of the liquid. Without removing her eyes from him, she moves her thumb to hit the send button:

    Of course I knew.

Dominic Jirak

ASH: THE HARBINGER

Ash, that particle, is the memory of those dreadful days—weeks—months. I do not recall how long it was—yet the doctors tell me that it was only a few weeks ago.

"Ash, what an odd—yet—beautiful particle. It is the one thing that destruction has neglected to erase. Yet it settles on the ground and gives nutrients to the soil." I freely muse this thought aloud, knowing that no one will bother a crazed man such as I.

"Bzzzzt—air raid—south front—bzzzt—casualties numbering over 500." The radio next to me blares the daily information streaming in from the war front.

A tired old doctor walks into my room, the room that smells like cleaner, blood, and sweat. He busies himself about the crowded room, checking on the dozen—or so—men laying in beds similar to mine. The radio continues its report, talking about areas in which I have no interest. I listen, however, for any news concerning Franz. Oh, how I hope the radio will stop soon. Will the report stop?

"—soreness today?" The doctor asked me something with a thick accent. I grunt, making a neutral reply, knowing the underlying question he is really asking.

Ash, it covers the land. You never find one ash particle by itself, do you. Yet, I recall, it seemed at first when I saw the first particle that it was only the one—nothing more, nor less—just the one. Yet, when I looked down, there laid the reason—how could ash settle with what had happened?

Franz—I saw him as I was carried to the truck. Did he survive? I saw him, but—maybe I did not—it does not matter, I blacked out anyways. I hope he is doing okay. He had a sister; his brother was fighting with us too.

"Bzzzzt—mortar fire—Montgomery Hill—bzzzt—heavy fighting but our forces prevailed." There it was, the radio mentioned the dreadful place, but my company moved from there—didn't they?

A soldier walked into my room, spitting on the floor. What a rude expression—what are those patches on his uniform? I don't recognize them—it does not matter. He must think we are cowards. I fought courageously—didn't I?

Machinegun fire, fire bombs, mines, barbed wire. I recall, that is what the world is. There is no beauty left, only those horrible sounds, the pound of cannons, the marching of boots, the firing of guns, and the explosions over our heads. We are soldiers. They tell us we are fighting for justice and security. All I experienced was ash.

Franz, he was such a nice boy—young—maybe 14 or 15. I looked after the kid, sparing my rations to allow him more food to survive the winter. It didn't matter if I died, I lived a life—him? Well, Franz was—is—such a young pup, hardly lived long enough to really start life. Yet, they stole it from him. How could a war fought with such young lives be fought for justice? What will be left but ash? Is that the security we are fighting for?

"Bzzzt—Mustard Gas attack on Montgomery Hill—Fifth Battalion requested reinforcements due to massive attack—Capt. Johnson is bringing his unit—bzzzt." Captain Johnson, I don't recall that name. Must be a new officer sent from the homeland.

One of the nurses came into the yellowing room. She is from the missionary service—the only people around this base that treats us as people. She brought stale bread and water to each of the poor sods within this disgusting, miserable, lonely room. God, bless her.

"You poor soul, have you had time to discuss with Fr. Richter?" The nurse asks me sweetly, hinting that a discussion with some clergy man would help alleviate my stress. How could it—does he have any knowledge of war, of the lengths that men will go to?

"Thank you, sister, I have not, though he needn't come, he is better off helping somewhere else." I respond, knowing that he will have nothing to say about Franz. Will he say that God will protect him? Bah, I have no need for such talk.

The nurse left in a hurry. She too, must not be able to stand this room without windows—the room that the doctors call "hopeless." These poor men know not of the fate that they are approaching. How sad.

Ash, the sky was covered with it when it happened. Yet around me and Franz, it did not fall—what happened there? Why did it happen? I did not see who did it—there was no honor—nor mercy for Franz.

Life is so similar to Ash. It drifts and floats about slowly, without a care in the world. No, Ash is more sinister than life—or maybe just as sinister—ash is the sign of decimation. It is grey and lifeless. Ash is what I recall. All I recall is ash.

"Bzzzt—Montgomery Hill has fallen—retreat in progress—command has requested the aid of nearby entrenched forces." The radio confirmed it, all that Franz and I fought for—all for naught. Are our lives so expendable? Did we take that hill for no reason? Why did we risk our lives for that hill which was not even defended?

The thunder in the distance rolls—sending an echoing noise through the building. I always loved storms—storms wash away the dirt and grime—they wash away the blood. Ash withers and dies in the rain—ash only disappears when water flows. This storm won't wash away the ash, though. I can hear the familiar whistle already. I hope Franz found peace. I hope the nurse survives this storm.

Ila Kumar

WHAT HE WANTS

 Arranged marriages and love marriages have the same percentage of working out, she says. He frowns.
 He doesn't know about rings, white dresses, or joint income. He knows heartbreak. He hasn't met patience but he knows waiting and being willing to do it again. He knows the first layer of skin coming off. He knows the second layer of clothing coming off.
 Akshay had just been told this statistic by his therapist, though at first, he thought she was only telling him this because he is Indian and they have a reputation for this kind of thing. Actually, what the therapist was trying to explain is that just because Akshay ended up going to college across the street from his house, that was no reason to conclude that his lost sense of agency would condemn him to four years of anguish. Fate may have given Akshay's college experience its savor of submission and disenchantment but he can still make it work just like everyone else.
 Without knowing anything about her hometown, he knows his therapist would never have chosen to go to college there. He doesn't know he's experiencing one of those rare moments in which truths sound like lies.
 It was Akshay's first time in therapy, and the woman sitting in front of him looked exactly as he had imagined on his walk from his dorm to her office: taupe sweater, smooth hair to her shoulders, bracelets that looked expensive. She looked related to the cast of Big Little Lies, a show his high-school girlfriend used to watch and talk about with her friends. Akshay's ex-girlfriend is named Ella. She had brownish hair with a crooked part and

talked a lot without saying much. If private schools had prom queens, it would have been her. She was so absorbed with herself, and Akshay always thought she should be more absorbed with him. Ella was at a mid-sized college across the country now. She was the prettiest Chi Omega he had ever seen. It was hard to believe that Ella, this carnival of good taste and physical beauty, was dependent on the whims of an institution filled with girls who rank themselves into tiers and boys who have a habit of groping their way through life.

When Akshay was seventeen years old and spending a lot of time with Ella, his dad would often drive to pick him up from her house. Akshay knew his father would listen to books on tape on the way to Ella's house, but on the way home, they would talk about writing. Akshay would tell him about books he'd read recently, and ask his dad what he thought about this person or that article. He wanted his father to think he was mature and responsible after he had just spent the last four hours doing nothing mature or responsible. In fact, Akshay often made his dad drive in rainy conditions, through summer hurricane warnings, or the snowy, deep blue liquid darkness of December. On the days when his mom would pick him up from Ella's house, she would always ask what they did. Akshay couldn't keep thinking of answers in place of the fact that they were really just learning about the sensations of impact and the way bodies smack and squeak and squish.

Akshay decided he needed therapy because he was undecidedly unhappy all the time. It was when he told his therapist that he was thinking about transferring schools, that she told him this bit about arranged and love marriages.

Akshay left her office that morning thinking hard about what she said. The day was cold, bright, blue. His father taught English at the college where he was now a student. Akshay had spent the last seventeen years and ten months of his life here. He didn't know physics. He knew even less about Keats. But he knew his first kiss, underneath a small tree across from the college's library. He didn't know where to put his hands, how to touch her lips and not her teeth.

The worst parts of his day are when he's not in class or in his room. When Akshay walks to class or eats meals—alone or with people—he fantasizes about marriage, about Ella, about the situation he's found himself in, and the things he could have done differently. He remembers sneaking into his first college party. He was sixteen. That night, he smoked his first cigarette with a couple of guys in his dad's class and walked home shirtless, scared the smell would get him caught. He remembers thinking, wow. This is so awesome. For some unknown reason, it doesn't feel awesome now that he was here.

Akshay walked back to his dorm room. He scanned his student ID at the door and walked up the staircase. He lived on the second floor of Abbot House. Akshay stepped into his room, relieved to see that his roommate was nowhere to be found. Without pausing to remove his shoes, he climbed onto his bed and laid his head down under his Ronaldinho poster. It was 1 P.M. With its thick walls, nailed-down floorboards, and heavy wooden door, the room around him felt solid and quiet. He fell asleep right then, his mouth dropping open, making the face of a gentle lover.

Akshay doesn't know much about arranged marriages. His parents got married when their two countries were fighting a war. His dad was born in India. His mom was born in Pakistan. When he tells people this story, it is usually around this time that the image of Cyril Radcliffe comes to mind. Akshay imagines this British lawyer—a man who had never before been east of Paris—tasked with partitioning the subcontinent in five weeks, using only a pencil and out-of-date maps. But when Akshay tells people this story, he doesn't mention Cyril Radcliffe. Instead, he tells them about how his parents met in New York and fell in love. He doesn't bring up the different diets, nuclear arsenals, and incompatible gods. Akshay says that it's actually a pretty funny story—my mom had set up her college friend on a date with my dad but it was my mom that my dad was actually falling in love with; how years later, they had him, and turned a bloody history into a baby boy and cello lessons, and Quaker school tuitions, and basketball tournaments, and runny noses, lost mittens, bad dreams, gas expended, babysitters, vacations, inside jokes, and please Dad, please let me sleepover!

And after all of this love was poured into him, here Akshay was, hating it all. What's that about?

Akshay had woken up. He picked up his phone and scrolled through Instagram. This did not make him feel better. The experience felt like ice skating for the first time: Akshay was immobile on the side of the rink, still struggling to tie his laces and the world was looping past him backward to show their smiles.

Ella had found herself a new boyfriend at college. He was hairy and looked like he smelled like a soccer field. Under the right conditions, he could be called good-looking. Akshay wondered if they did adult, college things. Did he come to her room at night and did she get up from her bed, smiling because she knew exactly what was going to happen when he walked through the door?

Akshay got up from his bed. He walked towards his window which overlooked the residential quad. The sky was overcast and aside from an elderly couple taking a walk, it was pretty empty. He stood and stared out the window, which was not unusual for bored college students, he hoped. Akshay dreamed about other worlds.

In this fantasy, he hits a deer turning into campus and calls his parents. Only his dad picks up the phone. His nose bleeds from the airbags and his dad brings a blanket to wrap around him. Akshay feels little again.

In this fantasy, he lives at home. He cooks elaborate meals with veal and squash and farfalle for his parents and they watch TV shows as they eat. He is too full to think about school. Sometimes at night, he hears whispering because his parents are worried about him. But then his mom says that she sleeps better knowing he is on the other side of her wall.

In this fantasy, he meets a girl at a party. They kiss just once and that is enough for her to go back to his room. He wonders what she will think of his Ronaldinho poster. He snapped out of it.

Quickly, it became clear to Akshay that it was Ella who had fallen into love marriage: a foreign, exciting territory made up of beautiful boys and beautiful her. She had successfully tapped into this mysterious current—college life: going out, learning French conjugations, and letting the age-appropriate boy drag his sweaty palm around her pretty knee. This felt so far away from him. In his arranged marriage, he didn't feel any of this enthusiasm. There were no roses and kisses and restaurant dinners in his marriage. What he really wanted was for the wedding service to be over, and for his wife to flatten out underneath his feet like a kitchen mat.

Claire McCarty

THE MOST PERFECT BIRTHDAY SURPRISE

The bell above the town hall struck two o'clock, that was Dr. Kristaps' que. He hung up his spotless white lab coat, revealing his drab brown shirt which he had meticulously buttoned to the very top, even though it was quite hot that afternoon; southern California usually is at this time of year. Today was the 15th of August but it was no ordinary day. It was a most glorious day. A day that had been planned methodically for the past 364 days. It was Dr. Kristaps' birthday. There was not a balloon or present in sight, and the only color that cheered up this dimly lit laboratory was a bowl of fruit, fresh off of the bursting trees of Dr. Kristaps' orchard. Dr. Kristaps reached out his long, thin figures and grabbed a beautiful apple, an action not uncommon for this peculiar fellow, and some hypothesized that his fancy, rather obsession, with fruit was the only commodity of this world that kept his resentful spirit on this earth. They were mistaken, however, for there was another love of Dr. Kristaps that he truly lived for, one that he would pine, long, and hope for as each moment ticked by, and today was the day he would satisfy his craving. Not a single soul knew the importance of that day and none cared to find out. They had learned long ago that this man, brilliant though he may be as a scientist, had not the faintest trace of human empathy to share. His attire always looked like he had just left the funeral of some dear friend, although everyone knew it could not be since he had none. Although he lived in this tropical climate his complexion matched that of the unforgiving snow of Antarctica. He would have passed by all unrecognized if it were not for his unique scar above his left eye, a burn mark whose origin remains unknown, but whose presence never goes unnoticed. One colleague overheard that it was from an accident with fire on one of his birthdays as a boy, but the story has never been corroborated. On his desk were two bottles of the finest Brandy, ones that he always treated himself to on this most wondrous day. He placed them carefully in a brown paper bag, glanced at his watch and was on his way. His destination, 742 Paramount Ave, was only a short walk away but his measured and deliberate steps had a noticeable energy to them.

    742 Paramount Ave was home to some of the most influential and important members of the community. If its prestigious board deigned to allow you to stay, it was a sure sign of your status and a high honor. In short, it was the apartments set aside exclusively for the rich and elite. Having grown up in less than favorable conditions Dr. Kristaps was so excited that it was the place of his favorite birthday celebration. He walked through the ravishing glass doors, through the elegant lobby, and to the elevator with chilling determination. As he waited, his eyes were fixed on the metal doors before him, but then his head turned, involuntarily as if pulled by some supernatural force to a woman sauntering towards him. He was caught off guard by her indescribable beauty, as if she were a descendant of the Greek goddess Aphrodite herself. She walked with poise and dignity in a maroon pencil skirt and matching blazer that were as rigid and chiseled as her jaw line. Her golden hair was in a perfectly tight bun, as if not a single hair dared to be out of place. As she approached their eyes met, although hers were as pure and blue as a wild mountain spring and his had a yellowish almost sickly hue. Her gaze immediately drifted up to his brutal scar, and remained there fixed. If she had been less focused on the disfigurement, she would have noticed his cheeks become rouge, not from love or embarrassment, but from rage. That anger like a wildfire consumed him, although he hid it well. Today was too significant to be derailed by this elitist. This woman lived in a kind of utopia, and knew nothing of suffering, of the labor it

took to get here today, of the hardships he endured as a boy, and she would not foil the festivities he had planned, of that he was sure. Although he tried to console himself thus, as they stepped onto the elevator he couldn't help but wonder what judgment was running through her mind. What disgust was hidden behind that heavenly smile, that clearly lacked genuine joy. She was perfect in every aspect. Every gesture, look and word were flawlessly constructed and faultlessly executed. They endured the 12 floor ride to the top of the Paramount Apartments, and went their separate ways, both hoping never to see the other again. Dr. Kristaps arrived at room 1226, enlivened and excited. The event room was a familiar place for he had frequented it every day for the last week and once a month for the past year. His birthday surprise was all prepared, only three other components were needed and his favorite day would be complete. First he walked exactly 14 and a half steps to a small red box that hung on the wall, and he pulled it. Immediately, alarms sounded and panic spread through these apartments like the plague. The street became flooded with the distraught residents of 742 Paramount Ave, a must needed audience for his birthday spectacular. Even though he had rigged the gas lines and ensured that this birthday gift would spread faster than joy to all, he wanted it to look like an accident, though one that, unlike his childhood, would not be forgotten. To this end he opened the two bottles of the finest Brandy and poured them haphazardly towards the point of origin. Then came the final and his favorite step. With zeal and a thrilling joy he reached into his pocket and pulled out a lighter, the only present he ever received, given as a joke but the legacy it had was no laughing matter. He enkindled the flame, a rush of intoxicating satisfaction set shock waves through his bones as this small flame grew, consuming everything in its path like a roaring lion mercilessly devouring its prey. One last time Dr. Kristaps looked out the window, and to his delight saw horror on the faces of the city's most powerful looking on from the street, as their most prized possessions stood at the mercy of the monster he created. He searched for one face, one who looked at him with condescending pity only moments before, but she was nowhere to be found. A minute of panic flooded his brain, was she not there to see his most glorious moment, the pinnacle of his success, the climax of his year? The smoke was now beginning to be insufferable, but he ran to the hall, knowing that her lodging was only a couple of yards away. The door of room 1220 was slightly cracked, and when he approached he was frozen in his tracks. There she sat like a statue carved by Michelangelo himself. She faced the door and calmly gazed out the window. The flames surrounded her but she did not stir, not a single muscle flinched. Her thoughts were running like a hamster on its wheel, round and round and round again. Her mind was inexhaustible, yet she longed for rest. She saw the fear on the faces of the people below, and their dismay lest they lose their money or assets. But what were they to her? Only a mockery, only a painful reminder. They were nothing but bribes to keep her quiet, and keep her existence unknown. She was not naive; she knew she was despised by her maternal grandparents, although the luxurious life she had was provided by them, not out of love but out of fear. Fear that their good name would be tarnished by the mistake of their daughter. Dread that their reputation would be stained if society knew that Greece's most affluent family had a scandalous granddaughter, born of a convict in Siberia. She led a life of opulence and grandeur but it was only a front for loneliness and despair. She had life indeed, but was she truly living? Alone, secluded, without a single soul that cared if she lived or died. Can this be called a life? Kristops knew far too well the look that seized her face, for he had seen it in the mirror many times as a boy. From it he was certain that she was resigned to stay. Though the flames consumed her, she would not move. For the first time he was confused about his intentions. He pulled the alarm well in advance so that no one would die. This was not the purpose or intent of his birthday surprise. He wanted to teach those who thought they were most important a lesson, not— no, it was not to kill them. As he beheld that figure of pain before him, not only did he recognize her sorrow, he felt her dejection and it shook him. Never in his life had he had a connection to someone, let alone one so powerful and real. He felt compelled to action. He rushed toward her, even though the smoke began to consume his sight and burn his eyes. He reached for her hand, it was numb, and the pure, blue spring of her eyes had iced over, yet they locked with his and this time did not wander. She spoke no words, made no gestures and yet he could hear her cry for help. He lifted her from the chair and began to make his way through the flames that by this time were omnipresent, consuming the building like one thirsty for revenge. As they escaped the ravenous fiend he had created, her eyes began to defrost by the faint flicker of hope enkindled by this fire, and he knew that what he once perceived as an insatiable monster would die with the flames that surrounded them.

Victoria Micha

(UN)HAPPY BIRTHDAY TO ME

There are two types of people in this world: those who hate their birthday and those who claim to hate their birthday. The latter claim to hate the attention but in reality crave it; they hate all of the expectations but only because they are never fulfilled. In reality, these types of people work hard to lower their expectation threshold to negative numbers; they set themselves up for failure. Every year when the two-month countdown begins, they silently pray that this year's celebration won't be an entire flop. Maybe this year that friend will actually remember to call. Maybe this year they'll make it on time for the dinner reservation. Maybe this year he'll deliver the letter that he promised. But it always turns out to be an over-inflated balloon that's bound to pop—and when it does, all it leaves behind is an annoying ringing in your ears. It helps to declare "I really hate my birthday," as if by saying it out loud, you are admitting defeat, and by doing this the Universe is bound to cut you some slack, right?
Wrong.

I say all this because I'm the second kind of birthday hater. I outwardly condemn that day of the year, while I silently yearn to have a good one. And to those who claim to enjoy their birthdays, what's there to look forward to? It literally marks one year less left in your life. Yes, bleak perspective but a true one nonetheless. Ironic that we're socially conditioned to think that birthdays are special days worth celebrating when, if you think about it, birthdays are a social construct to distract you from the fact that the clock of life is ticking, and you are not getting any younger. Humans were smart enough to counterbalance the sad truth about this day with an off-tune birthday anthem (also the most awkward moment of the day where the social etiquette makes it unclear whether you're expected to sing along or to smile and wait with an uncomfortable grin on your face) and a cake. We insist on marking this day as our most special of the year. If you ask me, this sure feels far from it.

 I'm smack in the middle of a booth surrounded on both sides—which means that there is no escape. My parents invited all of my "closest friends." I say "closest friends." I can't remember the last time I spoke to these people. When I look at their faces the only thing I feel is a sense of vague familiarity. I know them but I don't really know them. There's a shared past but a diverting future. I don't remember what school each one of them goes to or their major or the name of the new best friend they've made in school. I realize the last day I saw many of these faces was on the day of our graduation.

 Samantha, the girl sitting to my front and left asks "So, how is living in Chicago going?" I am too tired to remind her that I'm actually studying in Boston and not Chicago, New York, or Los Angeles, as other of my friends have suggested in previous conversations. I don't hold it against them, why would they care? This is one of those questions that a person asks without really being interested in a genuine answer. It's just a filler for conversation; what they're expected to ask, when in actuality I know their mind has gone elsewhere the moment I open my mouth to answer the question. They are just being polite. "It's been good. A lot of work but I've met a lot of cool people," my generic go-to answer. I spare them any and all detail that they most certainly don't want to hear. She mumbles a reply and we follow the conversation as it's picked up from the other side of the table.

 I don't tell them about my horrible roommate who sneaks her boyfriend in the middle of the night. Or that I've probably gained fifteen pounds from the horrible food from the dining hall. Or that seasonal depression has gotten me to an all-time low. Or that I fucking hate the snow. Or the fact that I'm still clinging to a long-distance relationship that's been hanging by a thread. Or the fact that it's been gettin harder to get out of bed and the only thing that I want is for him to call even though I know he won't. Moving away from home is far from the idealized story we are told. As far as they know, I'm living The Life.

 I try to make eye contact with my parents, the culprits of this birthday crime scene. They both thought it would be a nice idea to surprise me with a birthday brunch celebration the day after I arrived back for winter vacations. I wonder whether my brother was also a part of this. He probably was.

 Whenever someone asks what I like about having a male twin, I don't think about the built-in life partner or the telepathy kinks. I immediately think of the relief it is to share a birthday with your other half. The one thing that can help you feel better about yourself on the day of your birthday is knowing that you're not alone. So what better way for the Universe to lend a helping hand by sending me a twin? The perfect way to share the birthday burden.

 But this year, this is not working out. My brother is 9,518 miles away in the middle of an elephant reserve in Thailand. Which means that this year I'm all on my own. It's selfish, but I can't help but wish that he'd cut back on his travels and made it back on time for today. I finally make eye contact with my father and he motions a thumbs-up that I respond with a trademark roll of my eyes. It's weird seeing them together. Growing up, my birthday couldn't come fast enough. It was the day that fueled my sense of normalcy for the rest of the year. It was the day when we got to play the part of the picture-perfect family, a performance worthy of a TV ad. For a couple hours I could pretend that I wasn't the daughter of divorced parents. It's still a day that I always spend with the both of them but I no longer entertain my delusion of normalcy. After reaching a certain age I came to the realization that birthdays were just that: a delusion.

A day when people pretend. And that's why I'm suspicious of people who like their birthdays, they just love the delusion, love to entertain the idea that everything is perfect for a day when it is not. It is just an escape from their hard realities, and while that might be a helpful coping mechanism for some, it's a rather useless one because it has a twenty-four hour expiration date written all over it.

"Victoria, your phone."

My friend's voice snaps me out of my reverie. I look down and notice that I have a couple of unread messages. One's from an unknown number. When I changed my number after I moved last year I never got around to re-saving my contacts. That's how I know it's probably a text from a friend from my 'past life'. I don't bother asking who it's from or even reading what the text actually says. I respond with a "thanks for remembering" accompanied by a heart emoji. I re-type the same message for the second text.

I have a special dislike for birthday messages. They're more often than not a copy of a birthday template that you already saved on Notes. A corny and generic message that says a lot but doesn't mean much. It claims How good of a friend you've been or How wonderful of a person you are (really? wonderful?), and it more often than not comes from a person who I haven't spoken to in over a year, so how exactly am I a good friend? They ooze fakeness and have become so impersonal. Bottom line is I can't stand them.

I've always been terrified of people not showing up. It was always the case that friends would fail to show up or leave early for a "previous engagement". I was so insecure about it growing up that at one point I just stopped throwing any celebrations to avoid the anxiety. Anything to silence that little voice in the back of my mind saying that I wasn't worthy of being celebrated. I can't help but wonder who came for the sake of commitment and who genuinely wanted to see me. I do a mental scan and conclude that probably half of them are here for the wrong reasons. However, it calms me to know that at least my four best friends will be with me until it's over.

In between conversations I can't help but glance down at my phone. There's a three hour time difference which means that it's noon for him. He's bound to wake up any time now. It's the only birthday message I'm looking forward to. I realize that it is the first time in almost five years that I've spent my birthday apart from him. Now we have 9,000 miles between us and three time zones of separation. It was with him that I came the closest to not hating my birthday. I feel the tears pricking at my eyes but as soon as the first is about to fall I can see my mom approaching with a cake that says "20".

The other twelve or so people around the table join her in the chanting of "Happy Birthday," also known as the most awkward moment of the day. I plaster a dumb smile on my face and mouth a "thank you" to my mom, as I don't really know what else to do. With some help, she sets the cake in front of me and motions for me to close my eyes and make my three wishes. I close my eyes and blow out the candles:

I wish that he'd text me back.

I wish to always be surrounded by my family.

I wish that I'll make it to my next birthday.

Unhappy birthday to me.

VENUS FLY TRAP

    Students who come into the coffee shop in the evenings are the worst kind of customers. I don't say this as a mere opinion. I say it as a fact. They always come in, order a coffee—sometimes a pastry to go with it—and let it run cold. There's the tap tap of their fingers against the keyboard as they busy themselves with their latest gender studies or environmental science homework. They're fond of using words like hegemony and subversive. It isn't until I start getting the place ready for closing that they self-consciously pack up their belongings. They never leave a tip. Objectively, they're the worst kind of customers. Or maybe it's because they remind me of myself. Believe it or not I used to be a motivated college student. Now I serve lukewarm coffees and three-day old muffins for a living. I used to always fantasize about working in a coffee shop. The mechanics of working the coffee machine. Having easy conversations with regular clients. It all romantically appealed to me. But in reality the newness of these routines wears off rather quickly.

    I listen to the sounds of the morning rush, the soft hum of the refrigerator, the ding of the main door, the clatter of cups against plates, the laughter of friends who are deep in conversation. I always envision what their conversations are like. Are they discussing their latest weekend escapade? A date gone wrong? Or maybe the latest family vacation? I like making up these small stories in my mind. I imagine the couple sitting in the corner have been living together for a year. They bought a fancy Smeg toaster that is worth more than their mediocre salaries could ever afford. They're closer to his side of the family so they're planning to go to their country house to spend Memorial Weekend. I imagine the old lady who orders a decaf has a couple cats. Her house smells like mothballs and butter from the cookies that she likes to bake for her grandchildren. Her husband a victim to cancer. I imagine the girl on the phone is talking to her dad. Telling him all about her recent essay for her literature class. Her boyfriend hasn't texted in a couple days and she's worried he doesn't want her anymore. I imagine the two men sitting by the window are discussing numbers from their environmental start-up. One of them is a closeted reality TV fan and the other one takes piano lessons in his free time. Making up these stories satisfies my frustrated career as a writer.

    The *ding* announcing a customer snaps me out of my reverie. He asks for an iced latte. I find it a weird request since it's snowing outside. I scoop the ice, pour the coffee and top it with Borden two percent milk. "It's $3.50," I say. He mumbles a thanks and moves and settles into the furthest couch from the cashier. It's twelve on the dot when I have fifteen minutes. Time for my cigarette break. I grab my tote from under the cash register and head out into the back alley. I take an American Spirit from the pack and lean into the wall as I light it. The brick digs into my back and makes me remember the fire escape of my old apartment building. We would walk out on freezing Sunday mornings and talk about the previous night. Fog from our mouths mixing with the cigarette smoke. Fills me with the yearning to pick up the phone and call her. I run my hand through my hair and a clump of it comes off. My mom insists this is happening because of my hormonal changes. I know it's from stress. I hold on to it and bring it close for examination. Split ends the color of dry grass.

    A faint meow calls from the side street. "Hello Alyosha," I call out. I named it like my favorite character from Dostoyevsky's *Brothers Karamazov*. The brother who is infallibly good. Can't seem to get rid of the snobby lit major in me. As it approaches, I look for the bag of food that I keep hidden behind the trash. The meows become louder and more desperate. I dump some of it on the floor in front of her. My coworkers think it's a nasty habit, but I do it for the sentimentality. When I was young my mother would always feed the neighborhood cats. She would wake up before sunrise, when no neighbor was snooping, and fill empty dishes with food that smelt like day-old fish and wet paper. Sometimes she'd let us come close and pet them while they were too busy eating to care. She taught me to care. When I started noticing this little cat at work, I began buying Whiskas food and bringing it to work. We have conversations. I tell Alyosha about my life, and he gives me validation with his soft purrs.

"Finally got my severance deposited."

Meow.

"I should probably put it into my savings and not use it all up."

Meow.

"Although I still haven't picked up my shit from there. Whatever. They can deal with it."

Don't get a degree in English, they said. There's no real industry behind it, they said. Jobs in editorials are few and far in between, they said. Oh well, at least I can say I gave it a try. Or at least that's how I try to come off whenever someone asks me about it. I attempt to recall what things I left behind. A couple of Cliff bars, a packet of Bic extra fine pens, a red stress ball, chamomile and lavender calming tea, OPI Big Apple Red nail polish, chocolate covered espresso beans, a sewing kit, Neutrogena makeup remover, and a box of extra strength Advils. Nothing valuable. Let them deal with it. I put my cigarette out and step on the butt. "See you tomorrow," I call out to Alyosha.

As I head back inside, I'm mentally counting the hours left in my shift. Maybe I'll have time to send out some CVs by the end of my shift. Emails that go directly to avoid, never to be read or replied.

Usually this is the calmest time of the day. Everyone's at lunch and I have the place to myself. I dig through my tote back and find my copy of *Play It as It is* by Joan Didion. I find comfort in the relatability of the main character. The moment I open the book onto the dog-eared page I hear the door ding. As

I'm about to type in the order, I do a double take and involuntarily wince the moment I realize what's about to happen.

"Oh my god, Tessa! I almost didn't realize it was you!"

"Yeah, same I guess," I reply as I remember I have a coffee to prepare.

"Wait, I thought we weren't supposed to be here. Thought you stayed in Boston after graduation. I bumped into your mom a couple of months ago and she wouldn't stop talking about how you got a job at a hot-shot editorial company."

Her statement ends with a question mark, and I'm unsure if I want to reply. It takes me back to high school lunch break. It was the tone we used to subtly beg for more information without being direct about it. It irked me, this backhanded way of asking to know more. And that's the thing, in a small town like this everyone always wants to know more.

I silently curse my mom for allowing herself to engage in this sort of conversation, and for volunteering so much information about myself. I never seem to come close to the expectations others seem to have about me. And why do I even care?

I busy myself with the drink I'm preparing. Try to keep my eyes from staring at her annoyingly big 3-carat engagement ring. One. Two. Three pumps of vanilla syrup. I settle for a short "I did," as a curt reply.

I think about those slow motion animal documentary takes where the predator is slowly ambushing and catching its prey. I visualize myself as a tiny fly being trapped inside a Venus fly trap. Tiny teeth closing down on its prey. Venomous fluid secreted that slowly corrodes its victim. A slow and painful death. No escape. I'm the fly. Death is inevitable.

"Well...then what are you doing here?"

I couldn't answer the question. I just left her hanging in front of the counter with her iced coffee in hand. She's probably thinking I'm so rude, but who the hell cares. I glance up and down the alley as I'm lighting a cigarette with trembling hands. I hope he'll grace myself with his presence—my personal psychologist.

Meow.

I glance up and I can see his tail-waking from behind one of the big industrial trash cans. He senses me and immediately probably expects to get some food.

I take a long drag from my cigarette and exhale the smoke before my mental dam finally breaks:

"Alyosha. I. Do. Not. Know. What. I. Am. Doing. Here. I left this town only to be dragged back. She came into the shop only to remind me of everything that I had supposedly left behind. And then suddenly this ghost from high school is standing before me reminding me of everything that I wanted to leave behind. The keratin-straightened hair. Zara pleather pants. Freshly done manicure. Ugly Louis Vuitton emblem bag. The look that reminded me of everything I decided not to become. Everything that I left behind. And I'm angry. Seeing this cookie-cutter version of a woman in this town makes me angry."

Alyosha, who's been circling the trash bins finally takes a seat directly in front of me, he stares at me with what look like comprehensive eyes. That's enough confirmation for me to continue.

"They live a blissful existence secured by their planeness and naiveté. Waiting for the right guy. Move into the perfect home. Have perfect children. Life is figured out before they even know it. And that's the thing, I don't know if I would've been better off embracing the life that was perfectly outlined. Sometimes I feel like I only set myself up for disappointment. I dream too much. I want so much. And now I realize perhaps I was too naive to settle for a boring but comfortable life. Is there even value in what I have been doing? Because as far as I know, I'm much more miserable than them. I am much more tired than them. And I ended up here. Same as them. Probably more miserable than them, too. And that's the thing. There's a deep seated, insatiable need to find something that I don't even know

how to put into words. At least they can call it a ring, husband, bag, Maldives vacation, car. I. don't. know. And it makes me feel like I never will. My life will be an eternal quest for what?"
I say the last line with a hint of supplication. But supplication for what? I'm looking for answers from a cat. I think about how ridiculous this scene might seem to an onlooker.
Tic.
Tic.
Tic.
    I can hear the exalted rhythm of my heart. I feel like I have run a marathon. Maybe I have. A mental marathon.
    I look for some kind of reassurance in my therapist's eyes. An imperceptible nod of the chin. A tilt of the head. Nothing. So far there is nothing.
Tic.
Tic.
Tic.
    Another moment pregnant with expectation for an answer passes. Again, I forget that I'm talking to a cat.
    Meow.
    I recognize this last cry as a plea for food. I reach for another one of the hidden cans of tuna and open it up for Alyosha. He immediately goes to it and starts devouring it. I've lost all of his concentration.
    "So, tomorrow at one?"
    My question is answered by a definitive *meow*.

Kaylee Patterson

THE FACE OF DEATH

Tick…tick…tick

She breathed lightly on the lenses of her circular framed glasses and rubbed each one with her silk sleeves. She took a deep breath in and exhaled as she slid the spherical glasses up the bridge of her nose. Staring at her reflection in the mirror, her frizzy voluminous hair stuck out nearly six inches from her face.

Just another day at work, she thought as she cracked her knuckles. She touched up her red lipstick. Growing up in France, her parents were extremely devout Catholics. The Papacy didn't like makeup, and she didn't like the Papacy. She rubbed her lips together. It was the only color that shone against the grey concrete room with dismal lighting. It annoyed her that her psychiatry department could not seem to afford lighting of higher quality.

Tick…tick…tick

She noticed the clock in the high left corner of the room. It was time for her meeting, and she was never late. She walked down the cold stone hallway, her heels echoing like glass on marble. As she entered the interview room, the smell of bleach hit her nose. Cleaning days were on Monday nights. It was Tuesday morning.

"Good morning, Death. Are you ready for the interview?"

She sat down at her grey table. The room was lit only by a lightbulb from a singular lamp that hung above the table in the middle of the room. Death was leaned back in a grey metal chair. He wore a black suit with thin white lines running down and crisp edges. A shiny red tie slid down his chest, and a black fedora perched on his head. It was angled in such a way that a dark shadow covered his eyes and most of his face. Only a sharp jaw was visible. He kept his slouched demeanor and held a black cane with a gold knob at arm's length relaxed at his side. Although, she doubted he needed it because of his strapping physique.

She was ready to get this over with. Unfortunately, her lunch break was still three hours away.

"I consider it too early for it to be a good morning." His voice was low and raspy.

"Late night at work?" She sat down in her chair picking up her clipboard and number two pencil.

Merci. A wave of gratitude rushed through her as she noticed Frank, her favorite colleague, had set her a small foam cup of coffee on the table. No creamer. No milk. Only a single pack of sugar. Just the way she liked it.

"Yes," he replied.

"Mmm," she sighed, taking a sip of coffee. "So, you have been pretty busy working lately."

"Yes, and increasingly… today."

She nodded and picked up her clipboard. Her frizzy hair almost took over her spherical frames. "Okay Death, we can make this quick. I'm going to be straightforward and make this as simple as possible. I will ask you a series of questions that have simple answers that do not involve immense clarification. However, if you so wish, you may elaborate on your response and give further explanation. That will be solely up to you and at your discretion." Death remained impeccably still and did not give a response, but she was not expecting one.

In a single adjustment of her glasses, she looked down at her clipboard and cleared her throat. "Do you enjoy your field of work?"

"Only half of the time." She nodded and recorded the response on the thin piece of paper. "Is there any room for improvement? A promotion perhaps?"

"Such as?" he queried.

"Do you ever make mistakes doing your job?" She felt cold wisps of air caress her face as the air condition cut on.

"All the time. It's a tricky trade. Mistakes are certainly made."

"If you don't mind my curiosity, how?"

"Do you ever feel like you're falling when asleep at night?" Death opened his black-gloved palms. "I don't always wear gloves." He smiled wryly.

"Okay...okay," she said to herself as she jotted down the information. She had not taken note of his black leather gloved hands before. Interesting, she mused.

"Do you have to follow instructions of any kind? A manual, maybe?"

"Yes. I have to make sure I am thorough."

"If you don't mind my asking, why so thorough?"

"Because if a living human appears dead, putting them in a furnace for cremation can have dire consequences." He said deadpan.

"Noted." She scribbled onwards in her notes. "Now, what do you hate most about your job? Enlighten me."

"I hate being the bad guy." His jaw tensed, but he remained relaxed, holding his cane delicately at arm's length.

"Hmm, okay...alright." She made notes on the side of her margin. "Can you give me one example of that statement?"

"Everyone fears me. They wish I didn't exist, but I'm doing everyone a favor. You really want to live on this planet forever? Then go ahead and receive more pain and suffering than I will ever bring."

"Mm...okay, okay." She pressed down on her paper hard and took another sip of coffee. It was beginning to reach room temperature.

"Any stereotypes affiliated with your line of work you wish to put to rest?"

"People don't grieve me. They grieve their loved ones. They grieve the missed opportunities. The missed chances. They ruminate on all their mistakes; it must be exhausting. I am not dreadful. Only the perceptions I leave in my wake."

She nodded and filled in the lines on the form she filled out weekly. She had interviewed world-class criminals, the mentally insane, world leaders, and still, no one vastly interesting. "Most difficult part of your career?"

"People try so hard to stop me. They empty their wallets and go into debt trying to prevent me, but it's human knowledge and a fact that I will always come. Living is dying. Humans are like clocks. They are getting closer and closer every second until their precious time is up. If not now, then later. It is inevitable. I can only be delayed. When babies are born, I am already there. I wait."

"Your line of work must require a lot of patience then?"

"Extremely."

She swallowed the last bit of lukewarm coffee. "Well, now shifting gears. What do you like most concerning your career?"

"Seeing people ready for me. The ones that welcome me with open arms. The ones wanting to be done. Seeing people live a good life."

"It's quick, isn't it?" She drifted from her sheet. A little girl laughing prodded around her mind.

"Like that." He said while simultaneously popping his cane into the air and catching it with his gloved hand. "You know, I don't always have to be a bad guy. There have been many cases where I have taken people to a much better place really I—"

"What about the ones who are so young?" She cut him off.

"Well, those are the ones I feel sorry for the most. I hate taking them, and those that are simply not ready. They beg me, please just a little bit longer." He motioned outward, "I'm just doing my job."

She thought about the toys. All of which she could afford laying around the bedroom, mostly stuffed animals. She loved animals.

Remembering herself she looked down at her almost completed questionnaire which lay on the clipboard in between her hands. "Oh, umm. Do you have a boss or a manager even, to report to?"

"Yes."

She recorded the data, and he did not elaborate on the response. She didn't pry.

"Okay, Death..." She finished the sentence on her sheet and her pencil broke. Opening her desk drawer, another minute wave of thankfulness rolled through her as Frank had stocked her drawer with four other number two pencils. Merci beaucoup.

"We are almost done here..." She clicked her tongue against the roof of her mouth as she skimmed down the paper. "Okay, do you get let's say... free will in your position, or are you merely given orders that must be fulfilled." She thought of her. She was just a jeune fille.

"I don't have much free will, but of what I do I use it rarely."

"Such as?" again she had forgotten herself and zoned into the shadow underneath the fedora. The grey concrete walls disappeared from her vision into the black oblivion shadows that painted their corners. It was morning, but the darkness mimicked minuit.

"Sometimes I give people a little bit longer, but sometimes I take people a little bit quicker."

She waited for further explanation, but none came.

"Why? Why do you do that? What motives govern you to do such actions?" Her voice cracked.

His gloved hand gripped the golden knob of his cane tighter. "I do what will be best in the grand scheme of things. Although, in most cases, people never see that."

Tick...tick...tick.

The wall clock marched on.

She swallowed hard. "Last question. What would it be if you could give any advice you have learned from your field of work?" She heard her again in the back of her mind. Memories she shoved far and away. She heard screaming. She heard, Stop!

Mommy, Stop!

He began to rise. "To live. You only get one shot." He tipped his fedora toward her. He held his cane out to his side and started to stroll out of the room; the cane placed in hand but only aiding in his perfect gait.

Without any knowledge or reason, she stood up in a start. "Why did you take her!"

He stopped.

"She was only six! She wanted to be a veterinarian! She always asked Mommy do you want to play with me? But I always told her later because I had work or…or was tired. I was an interviewer that worked late and past time, no over hours!" She choked on her words. "Well, later never came!" Her head was pounding, and emotions flooded her chest.

She had initially spent many days not grasping her daughter's death. She kept her daughter's room tidy expecting her to rummage around and play again. She kept her stuffed animals situated around the play table for a tea party just the way her daughter liked. The only thing was, she never came back. Days flooded into nights where she would cry herself to sleep. She thought being unconscious would alleviate the pain, but it only brought back the memories. Upon awakening, the sudden onset of heavy dread hit her stomach with reality after being numb to emotion would be even worse, and it brought on the hardest tears.

"I am not always able to follow the plan. I often have to heed to the beckoning calls of others…" He slowly turned around.

She looked into the deep shadow to where his eyes would have been. He slowly leaned his chin up, and she saw features slowly come to light.

Tick…tick…tick

The scene flashed across her memory. She had been drinking. They left the party late. The party horns. "Happy New Year!" That phrase reverberated off her stomach with nausea. The rain. The traffic. The lights. She was going fast. She remembered the heat turned on in the car. She remembered swerving across the glassy street.

"Mommy, are we almost home? Can we stop, please?"

The screeching. The slam into what felt like stone. The broken glass, and the painful somersaults. The slicked blood. The hospital waiting room. Those blue stitched chairs. The nurse with black hair that swam over her shoulders in coils.

"I'm so sorry your daughter is gone. She died on impact. I am so sorry."

It all came back to the forefront of her mind. Death's facial features were now seen clearly in the dim light. She saw spherical glasses and a slender nose. She saw frizzy hair. She saw the spitting image of herself staring back at her.

Tick...tick...tick...

She awoke in the asylum. Her arms wrapped around her. She fought trying to untangle them from her body, but her arms would not budge. She buried herself against the padded floor. She had another fit. This time it was bad. It seemed even more real. The lights were too bright. Frizzy hair was plastered to her face in sweat, tears, or saliva. Probably all three. She needed her glasses. Everything was blurry.

A hazy figure entered through the padded door. She squinted as it moved closer. Her vision began to clear as the psychiatrist in shiny red heels walked toward her.

"It is time to get up, Ms. Anthony."

Rachel Patterson

ILL-FATED

A man lay dead on the cobblestone path in the most peculiar way. His veins were drained dry, and his corpse was hollow. It seemed like he had been there for many weeks while the townspeople simply walked over his decayed body to go about their day. But that was not the case.

In this town, the people are poisoned, or possibly cursed. It might be something in the wine, the wind, the threads of their clothes. They know there is something lurking amongst the town; someone who disrupts their passive way of life. Despite the recent horrors, the people only dig their graves and hope they will not fill them for many years.

***

Like everyone at the ball, Susan didn't think of the most recent death, or what tomorrow's sun would bring. She only thought of tonight, and the midnight moon that told stories of strangers in love.

The ocean of bodies before her, where the dresses—most stitched by her own hand with her finely spun silk—shimmered like waves rolling to shore. Susan felt the tide of them pull and beg her to join them in their maenadic trance. But she was looking for someone, and she could not dance until she found him.

The Spring Ball was set in the middle of town where celebrations had taken place for many months. There was a large field with a makeshift dance floor that was surrounded by a border of hedged mazes and secret paths. Susan wove between lone-standing, white pillars and large vases of flowers. Everything was veiled in the gold of candlelight and half-shadowed from the vast blackness above. It was the last dance of the season, and the only one Susan had attended. Many people were surprised to see her there. Everyone knew her family thrived off the business these celebrations brought in, but Susan and her sisters were never invited to join. She'd only been invited tonight out of pity. She was alone, after all, since her sisters had abandoned her.

The dance was beautiful, and the air felt stimulating. Susan prowled between bodies and plotted careful steps as if to protect a fragile floor while she searched for Augustus. She had become accustomed to sneaking when it came to him. It had been months now of window visits and whispered glances across open spaces filled with hundreds of faces in town that never noticed a thing. Susan convinced herself she didn't mind that their love wasn't public. She told herself quite often that, in love, sacrifices had to be made.

She caught a glimpse of Augustus nearing one of the garden mazes now, and just before he disappeared between its walled shadows, he glanced over his shoulder.

Had he seen me? He must have, she thought.

She grabbed two fresh glasses of wine from a nearby table and turned to follow, but someone ran into her shoulder and sent the wine tumbling.

"Oh, my dear! I am so sorry!" It was Georgette and her pack of wolves. The golden girl of the town; the governor's daughter. Midas had blessed her with more than the material wealth her family liked to flaunt. Her skin and ringleted hair were a shimmering sunrise.

Susan looked down at her once lovely gown. The wine spread deep red across the sage green of her chest like a bullet wound to the heart. She caught glimpses of passersby as they stared with suppressed smiles. The townspeople knew how to stay out of Georgette's way; they knew even more about the speculations against Susan's supposedly murderous family. No one was willing to help, and some likely enjoyed the humiliation. There was nothing more entertaining than to watch the puppet master pull at Susan's strings.

"You look lost here all alone. Where's that little 'Angel' you're usually dancing around town with? Her and Holly didn't want to join you at the ball?" Georgette gave a mock pout.

"Holly and Angelica are out of town on an errand," Susan replied. She gripped the empty glasses in her hands. She could only think of how natural they would look embedded in Georgette's pretty head.

"That's what you said last week. And the week before. Poor thing," Georgette said. "They left you, didn't they? All alone to take up the family business? They realized how useless of a life they were living, but couldn't bother to drag you along, I suppose." She turned to her pack and giggled. "I heard a little rumor…something about your sisters. With all this death, it's peculiar they scurried from town so quickly, don't you think?"

Before Susan had a moment to defend her family, Georgette turned and began to walk away. Susan gripped the wine glasses even tighter and stared at a golden ringlet where it bounced at the back of Georgette's head, but after a moment she set the glasses aside. She wouldn't become the monster everyone suspected her to be. Although Angelica and Holly would likely be overjoyed.

Susan tried to wash out the wine, but instead she smeared it more along her chest. Eventually she gave up and followed Augustus into the garden. Hopefully he wouldn't mind that her dress was no longer beautiful like all the rest.

The thought of Augustus always made Susan feel like a sunrise. He blanketed the cavernous depths of her heart in a warm light, and she plunged willingly into that golden web of clouds. From the bottom of her heart, Augustus looked to be flying. She knew she would jump again if he ever asked her to. This is love, she thought to herself. To give everything you are, and everything you ought to be, to another. And she truly believed it was. Out of everyone in the world, she held onto him; the one who grounded her, who kept her sane among the chaos that so often clouded her brain. It is why she had chosen him over her family when they left her behind. Her sisters never made her feel anything but cold and unforgiving.

Between the arborvitae walls of the maze, familiar and unwelcome whispers drifted to Susan. She felt many eyes on her—her sisters. They seemed to say they knew something she didn't, a secret Susan refused to acknowledge. Further in, the maze grew dark, the green became thick, black shadows that stretched overhead. She caught glimpses of Augustus around corners before he quickly faded from view.

"Augustus," she whispered. It came out giddily, as a schoolgirl might call after her classroom crush only to turn and tease in a game of chase. That was what he was doing now, wasn't it? A game of chase? How romantic that was, for him to lead her to the depths of the maze, to the hydrangeas at its center. There he would grab her waist in a fit of passion—two lovers together in the garden where forbidden lovers have always met.

At the center of the maze were two figures caught in a fit of passion, just as Susan imagined they would be. But it was not Susan and Augustus, only Augustus and someone else.

She knew Atlas had faltered when the ground shifted beneath her feet. On the horizon now, the heavens no longer aligned with the mountain peaks, and the rivers had altered their course. All along Susan's world had been distorted by Augustus' false light. From within the garden walls her sisters whispered that she should have listened to their warning.

Susan ran out of the maze, towards the exit that led away from the party. Here there were no herds of warm bodies or high garden walls to keep the fog from rolling in, only the evenly spaced corpses deep in the graveyard a few paces away. She feared for a moment their souls might linger in the place that wreaked so violently of death. Despite this she ventured through. It was the fastest way home, even if it seemed the most frightening. From the tree line beside her, she heard the same familiar movement from the maze. They were following her now, always watching. Susan quickened her pace while she squinted into the darkness ahead and willed the silver haze to keep its constant cover. Some things were better kept secret.

Someone grabbed Susan's wrist and she screamed. She tried to pull away, but his grip was too strong. He said something she couldn't hear over her frustration, but finally, he let go. The force of her desperation dragged her to the ground, but within a moment she was pulled to her feet.

"Listen to me Susan!" Augustus shook her shoulders.

"Did it mean anything to you?" Tears bit the base of her throat.

"Susy," he whispered, and she wasn't sure why. The dead didn't have ears. If they did, they would be filled with worms and maggots by now. He reached for her hand. She let him take it.

"I wish I could say something better, Susy. But the truth is, you're only a seamstress. Georgette's family is so rich she's practically royalty. How could I not marry her?"

The headstones grew beside her, or maybe she shrank in size. She was trapped in a concrete tomb with Augustus' words carved deeply along every inch of the walls, like an epitaph that encircled her for eternity.

"Georgette," Susan repeated. "You're marrying Georgette?" She dropped his hand.

"Yes, soon. We are announcing it tonight. I swear I didn't know you would be here."

"Is that supposed to make me feel better?"

Augustus ignored her comment, "It has been planned between our families for quite a while. I probably should have told you sooner."

"Probably—"

"What you and I had," he continued talking over her, "it

was a fit of lust. We were never meant to be anything more. You had to have known I couldn't marry you. Look at how the town talks of you, and how vicious they can be. It is dangerous just to be seen with you. They will use you as a seamstress, take every advantage of your kindness and ability, but they will not hesitate to burn you down should you show them a reason."

"They are not the ones who took advantage of me," Susan said. Once she thought she held his heart, but now she only held her ground. She continued, "Call it what you like, but for me it was not lust."

"Well, this doesn't have to be the end—"

"Yes," she said firmly. "I may despise Georgette, but I will not settle as your secret seconds any longer. Best of luck in your endeavors, Augustus," she said, and watched him disappear beyond the hedges to the liveliness on the other side.

She thought this feeling would never end—this aching pain that had blossomed in her chest and skipped along her bones. It wrapped her chest in thorny roses and pinched, but not tight enough to burst, only enough to become unbearable. Through it all, her heart ticked proudly against her agony, and she willed it to give up the stubborn consistency. Under her breath she cursed them both; cursed Georgette's beauty and Augustus' charm and the stars that must have fallen from heaven to bless the golden skin where his lips would linger. She silently cursed Angelica and Holly too from wherever they hid now.

The party died down, and Susan walked the rest of the way home alone. The shop felt bigger and emptier than ever before, though the presence of her sisters lingered along the walls and in the many dresses they stitched months ago. Susan tried to busy herself with new work and ignore the thoughts that crept into her brain. Despite the agony, she held tightly to the hope that Augustus might knock on the door. Maybe he would say it was a mistake, and that he loved her all along. She would take him back because he made her feel human and so different from the rest of the hollowed people that wandered this cursed town. Her monstrous sisters too.

Susan fought valiantly against the ache in her bones and the stretch of her skin. In the sharp ridges of her spine, she could feel her body begin to transform. She refused to shift; she would not become something to fear. But so little effort would be required to make them pay. The town walked by while Georgette kicked her to the ground; they stood resolute while her sisters picked their neighbors one by one, and never acknowledged the truth out of fear or selfishness or lack of care. Augustus was right, the town needed her abilities. How could they host a grand ball without pretty dresses? Without her, celebrations would be put on hold. The town might begin to realize how much power Susan held over them. Yet, Susan was not a monster. She would wait, and Augustus would come. She would take him back because she deserved the happy life he offered. She would stitch dresses for the rest of her days and watch the town throw their worries away with drink and dance.

A knock at the door shifted the stale air of the shop. Outside the day was bright, and she began to wonder how long she'd locked herself in. It could have been days, or maybe weeks spent in the storm of her mind.

It was not Augustus, but Georgette who swept into the shop without invitation. She talked of her wedding dress, "Champagne colored…no, ivory! With lace," while Susan simply stared, still as stone. Georgette dragged her hand along every dress in the shop before she landed upon one Angelica started long ago.

"This one," she said. Susan only heard Angelica's voice, *Finish it, and bring them to the ground. Make them beg for forgiveness. They'll wish they hadn't thought so lowly of us, asked so much of us, expected us to sit back idly with false content while they danced over our toes and played with our feelings.* She realized that Augustus wouldn't come, he made his choice long ago. Now his bride was here to suck the last human life from Susan's bones, drain her heart of all she had left to give.

Susan took the unfinished garment from Georgette and smiled. Yes, she would make Georgette a dress. A lovely one; the perfect one. After months of hesitation, Susan was finally ready to join the family business. So, she pulled the threads, and like puppet strings, they followed her will. She sewed each detail in place, right down to the last speck of dirt that would cover their bones. They had already dug their graves; it was her business to fill them.

In only a few days the details were finished. Susan knocked on the door of the governor's mansion. Her bones ached deeply, and her heart was sore, but she was still able to offer the dress to Georgette with a smile. She stepped aside for Susan and the two of them entered the dressing room. Susan sat and waited while Georgette disappeared behind the changing screen with her lovely new dress in hand.

"No hard feelings?" Georgette said. Her arms peaked over the top of the screen as she slipped into the fine silk.

"None at all," Susan responded.

The pain in joints told her Georgette had put on the dress and the transformation had begun. When Georgette walked from behind the screen, Susan's smile cracked wildly across her cheeks. Georgette admired the way the dress complimented every curve of her figure. The shape grabbed at her hips and squeezed her waist just a tinge. The ivory color made her hair seem more golden than ever before. And as for her skin—oh, her skin! The color brought rose to her cheeks as her pores bloomed with fresh blood that began to stain the pure dress. Georgette turned to Susan, she reached, but her hand fell away as her arms became frail. She bled on the ground, and Susan watched until the job was done; until Georgette's figure had become red skin and bones, and all that remained was a hollow husk where beauty once stood. Susan felt the last of Georgette's lifeline ease away and soak her bones instead. This was why her sisters killed. The power was refreshing.

Susan strolled out of the house, and down the street. The

pain was excruciating now while her skin stretched, and her spine twisted. She barely made it to the shop in time to collapse.

Susan covered the windows. The townspeople had begun shouting outside the shop not long after she returned. She heard one voice clearer than the rest. So, he had come back for her. In the shadows she waited for them to tear through the door and fly into her trap.

Augustus entered first, followed by the rest of the town. The men and women, so keen to sit back before, now held torches and weapons and stood at the ready, more than prepared to take matters into their own hands.

"Find her!" Augustus said. Lanterns sent the shadows of hanging dresses into motion around the townspeople like a deadly dance. It was Susan's private ball, and it was kind of them all to accept her invitation. She paced quietly nearby, but when they found no one, the townspeople began to turn their thoughts to new possibilities. Some told Augustus he was crazy—no woman could plot a murder that cruel. Someone simply whispered, "She probably fled from town with her sisters. It's no use to track them now."

"Besides, there might be a curse on the town, and what are we to do? We are months too late. Why act on it now?" another questioned.

"Or maybe it's simply the fate of the deceased and we have nothing to fear now that this wretched family is gone," said someone at last.

Augustus turned to them, "Yes, it must be a curse and it must be fate and she must be somewhere! So quit speculating and find her!" He raised his fist and Susan simply rolled her eyes. "All these months spent in fear of the next death. In fear of this hysterical, madwoman plotting against us all!" The room nodded in agreement. Augustus stood tall but Susan was taller. "She has taken good men," Augustus continued, "strong men. She has taken your brothers and your sons. Your daughters, sisters and…wives. She will not take another soul. Today we take fate into our own hands, and we no longer sit back in fear. We must find her; we must put an end to this cruelty. And you must believe me. You must trust me."

"Trust?" Susan liked the way her voice echoed across the room. "Trust you?" The townspeople turned in circles. They could not see Susan, though they were perfectly in her view. "All you wonder is true, and you may call us what you will: a curse, fate, hysterical, mad. But we are not cruel, not really. Although, we may be slightly devious. Call us Justice if you like. Indulge in our wine, bathe in our sweet nectar, but do not be mistaken. Our hand is steady, and we do not tip the scales. It is your own gluttony that fattens you, our only job is to weigh you like the prized pigs that you are."

"She's in the rafters!" one man yelled and pointed a finger to Susan's great shadow. Someone shattered a lantern, and the silks quickly caught the flame. Around the shop came a translucent shimmer, at first thought to be a trick of the eye, but then they seemed to notice: thousands of webs across every rafter and layered so thick they blocked the windows. Some townsfolk tried to run, but got caught in the glimmering, sticky strings. Their fear was pungent.

Susan dangled from the rafters then; her egregiously plump and fleshy body a true horror to behold. Her sisters emerged too from their spiral burrows along the walls. Holly looked dark and devious while Angelica moved silently among the shadows. The fire shone playfully across the fine hairs of Susan's many legs and illuminated the twenty-four eyes that continuously circled the ceiling and walls of the burning shop. For the first time since the maze, Susan felt beautiful like her dresses from the ball. She knew now that she should have given into her true nature long ago.

The three women worked in calculated unison to measure each body, spin their length of thread, and cut their fate a little short. They hung each hollow corpse above the flaming pyre that now covered most of the old wooden floorboards. Every lifeline drained made the women more powerful.

Augustus pleaded when Susan finally approached him. He dropped his weapon and knelt to the ground, "It was you, Susy. It was always you who I loved, never Georgette." She only laughed. Augustus stayed still, a cowardly statue under Susan's stare. She quickly got him by the legs. An animal plea escaped his throat as splinters wedged beneath his fingernails and broke calluses on the skin of his hands while he clawed at the ground, desperate for something to hold onto. He begged, "Spare me! Please, show mercy!" Mercy. That word seemed unfamiliar to Susan. Distant. Trapped alongside her human heart, in the garden labyrinth that stood miles away.

She did not have to wait for town gossip to know Augustus' fate. There would be no field of flowers in his place, no grand hero's tale, and no survivors to speak the legend of the man who led an entire town to despair. Susan simply tucked him tightly in her silky cocoon and dragged him into the dark woods where they could finally be alone.

"Only a seamstress," Augustus had said to her before. If he had once been ashamed of her title, he had nothing to be ashamed of now. She was so wealthy in power that she was practically royalty. It was a dead town now, a cursed town, and she would rule them all.

Austin Schwartz

LANTERN'S LIGHT

    Christina Graff was sitting in her art studio. Well, what she considered her studio. Her father rented out a storage unit once she moved out of the house. Little did he know that she had sold most of her belongings to try to make ends meet as an artist in Seattle. She lived in Renton on the outskirts of the big city and every day she would work as a Starbucks barista from open to noon. After that she'd skip lunch and try to sell her art to any big wig she could hold the attention of for more than a few seconds on their, what they might call, casual stroll to the next meeting. After an hour of sales pitches, she would go to the storage unit and work on new paintings until deep in the night. She had a cot there, sometimes she would get so captured in her newest project that it would be well into the morning before she went to bed, so it made more sense to stay instead of head back to her apartment.
    She wasn't a bad artist by any means. The problem was most of her work fell under what the unappreciative called modern art. "Nothing but brush strokes of random color," many would say when showing off her pieces. These people weren't thinkers. They were the monotonous business folk of the modern society. Industrialization is great for progress, but appreciation of creativity is lost in the smoke.
    To Christina, her paintings were more than abstract compositions. They featured the inner secrets of the cosmos; the liquid gears within a being's soul connecting every individual to a greater universe. There was a higher power out there, but what it was belonged to eyes that none of us could see through, it was stardust pupils and blazing retinas of flame. A beauty that took

eons to understand. A level of comprehension that no one could have ever known, not even her who painted it. But little did she know that she would come closer to knowing the secrets of the universe than anyone else on Earth.

Christina Graff knew of the Justice League and many other heroes who rose to battle crime. Yes, they were heroes, she understood that, but strip away their power and they are just like her. A big heart and willingness to persevere, that's why she didn't praise them like everybody else. "Gods Among Men," she had heard it so often over the radio when working it caused some of her pieces to flourish red with rage. "Men among men," she would say. Then she'd scoff, "women among them too."

Miss Graff didn't expect a time that all the channels cut to the same news story. It had been a stressful day. She overslept at her studio and was late to her shift at work for the sixth time that month. The sympathetic viewer would have found it too harsh, but in the real-world business must keep moving and her boss had fired her that day. Back at her studio she had been splashing paint across her canvas with no vision in mind. Her anger only pointed toward herself for not being as disciplined as she would like. Her rage only grew when she continued to flip through radio channels for music to feed her frenzy and all she could find was "breaking news." But she dropped her tray on the floor when she heard what devastation had altered every broadcast.

"A battle in Star City, California. Superman and the rest of the Justice League were able to defeat the villain known as Parasite, but before apprehending the criminal the Green Lantern perished. As far as sources know the criminal went to absorb the Green Lantern's power, but instead claimed his life source. No JLA members have come forward to comment on his loss at this time. I'm Louis Lane and thank you for listening to the Daily Planet."

What most don't know is that Parasite didn't intentionally kill the JLA member, though I'm sure he wouldn't have minded doing so. Parasite wanted only to absorb the Green Lantern's power thinking he could conjure something on his own to fend off the rest of the JLA; however, like most Americans he had assumed that Green Lantern possessed his own power. Only a select few heroes outside of the Core itself knew that the power of a Lantern comes from the ring they wear, thus Parasite was unable to absorb the power of the Green Lantern. It was Batman who first approached Reiner's body to claim the ring. Not because he wanted its power. He knew that it was the ring that held it and wanted to keep it from falling into the wrong hands, when suddenly it vanished. Batman believed it was at sonic speed, but the Flash wasn't there for him to confer if it truly disappeared or began to travel.

"Holy shit!" was all Christina could say, astonished that she was right. These heroes were just as human as anyone else when suddenly a sharp pop rung throughout her studio. She turned at the second of the sound, but in that moment, she realized her feet were no longer touching the ground. She was hovering in the air.

A green light began to paint itself across the room as a single thought came across her mind, "In brightest day, in darkest night, no evil shall escape my sight. Let those who worship evil's might, beware my power, Green Lantern's Light!"

She uttered these words, and her head was thrown back as green light glazed across the room knocking all her work to the floor. Paint splattered across the room leaving red, orange, blue, violet, and yellow across the walls.

DRAMA

Cynthia Chen

CHARLOTTE AND AMELIA

<u>CHARACTERS</u>
CHARLOTTE
AMELIA

<u>SETTING</u>
Café - Day

It's Sunday morning. The sun is shining and people are smiling. Charlotte and Amelia walk hand in hand into a café and sit at a two-person table near the front bay windows. It's their usual spot. There's a glass cup on the table with six sprigs of daisies. Faint jazz music is playing. They settle into their seats, then look up and face each other. Amelia is smiling but trying not to.

>CHARLOTTE
>(skeptical) What's wrong?

>AMELIA
>(smiling) Nothing's wrong. Everything's fine.

>CHARLOTTE
>You look well. And happy. Something's up.

>AMELIA
>(smiling bigger) Shouldn't you be happy that I'm happy?

CHARLOTTE
I am. I am. I truly am. But I also want you to know that this new you? (waves in the direction of Amelia's face) Is a bit scary. You look happy. *Too* happy. This is not us.

AMELIA
It's my birthday. Maybe I'm just happy to see you.

CHARLOTTE
Maybe you are.

Charlotte keeps staring at Amelia as she looks down at the daisies.
Amelia picks one out of the cup and plays with it. Twirling it between her fingers and watching it spin.

AMELIA
(a beat) Fine. I met someone.

CHARLOTTE
You met someone. Does he have a name?

AMELIA
Yes, but you're not going to know it.

CHARLOTTE
(narrows her eyes) Why? Is it because he's ugly?

AMELIA
(stares at Charlotte)

CHARLOTTE
Fine. It's because he's boring and you know I'll hate him.

AMELIA
He's very interesting, if you must know.

CHARLOTTE
So we're back to ugly.

AMELIA
So we're back to nothing because we're not going to talk about him. We're going to have a nice breakfast with good coffee and enjoy this beautiful morning.

CHARLOTTE
You're boring. And you're buying. I'm going to order the most expensive thing on the menu.

A waiter comes over to take their orders. Charlotte orders an egg benedict and hot black coffee. Amelia orders strawberry pancakes and an iced latte. Their usuals. They go back to staring at each other. Amelia smiles again.

AMELIA
You look very nice today.

CHARLOTTE
I look nice every day.

AMELIA
I know. I just wanted to tell you anyway.

CHARLOTTE
Thank you. Anyway.

Charlotte interlocks her hands and places them beneath her chin. Then stares at Amelia with doe eyes and blinks twice.

AMELIA
(a beat, then sighs) His name is Finn.

CHARLOTTE
(smiles) I knew he had a name. What else?

AMELIA
No.

CHARLOTTE
No?

AMELIA
(a bit defeated and exasperated) No, because he's a very nice guy and he's funny and I like him very much so we're not going to talk about him because you're just going to find something about him that's a little bit odd and we're going to overanalyze it and I'm going to hate him by the end of today.

CHARLOTTE
(a few seconds pass) I don't do that.

AMELIA
(stares at Charlotte)

CHARLOTTE
I don't *have* to do that.

AMELIA
(twirls the daisy then lifts it to Charlotte's face and points at her)
You promise?

CHARLOTTE
If you like him, I'll like him. (a beat) I'll learn to like him. I promise.

AMELIA
But I can tell when you're lying.

CHARLOTTE
But at least I'll be trying.

AMELIA
I love that you do.

CHARLOTTE
And if he's truly a good guy and a good match for you, I'll like him. Really.

AMELIA
You know I usually have pretty bad taste in men.

CHARLOTTE
I plead the fifth.

AMELIA
I know you know I have bad taste.

CHARLOTTE
Then why are you asking me about it?

AMELIA
I'm not. I just want you to know that Finn's an exception.

CHARLOTTE
Sure. (singsongy) I'll believe it when I see it.

AMELIA
You're insufferable sometimes.

CHARLOTTE
Yet you keep coming back for more. (a beat) Okay, let's talk about something else now. We're not passing the Bechdel test.

AMELIA
We're not in a movie. Also, you're the one who asked about Finn.

CHARLOTTE
And now we're going to stop talking about Finn.

The waiter comes over, carrying the black coffee and the latte, and sets both drinks on the table. Then, they walk away.

CHARLOTTE
How are you?

AMELIA
(smiles) I'm good. You?

CHARLOTTE
Eh. Could be better.

AMELIA
I don't think I've ever heard you say you're doing good. Just good.

CHARLOTTE
Because it can always be better.

AMELIA
That's true. (a beat) Are you unhappy?

CHARLOTTE
A little. But I'm always a little unhappy.

AMELIA
So no more than usual.

CHARLOTTE
Well, maybe a little more than usual. But not by too much. Nothing you need to worry about.

AMELIA
You shouldn't be. It's my birthday. We're basically the same person so it's like your birthday too.

CHARLOTTE
That's not how it works but I applaud your effort for trying.

AMELIA
Then give me your worry as a gift. It's my birthday anyway. Nothing will bring me down. I'll just take your worry and it'll evaporate as soon as it touches me.

CHARLOTTE
That's so kind of you.

Charlotte picks up another daisy from the cup and gives it to Amelia. Amelia puts her daisy down on the table and takes Charlotte's daisy and quickly chucks it to her right. The daisy hits the window and falls back onto the table. Amelia covers the daisy with her hand.

AMELIA
See? It's gone.

CHARLOTTE
(smiles and sighs contently) And I feel so much better.

The waiter comes to the table again to bring the food. They drop off the plates and ask if they need anything. Charlotte and Amelia both say no. The waiter leaves. Charlotte and Amelia resume their conversation.

                CHARLOTTE
       Controversial opinion on a topic?

                  AMELIA
(contemplates for a moment) I like pineapple on pizza?

                CHARLOTTE
          Too nice. You're too nice.

                  AMELIA
             I'm not. You?

                CHARLOTTE
        I have one. (takes a bite)

                  AMELIA
                Yes?

                CHARLOTTE
(chews and covers her mouth to speak) You won't like it.

                  AMELIA
          You always say that.

                CHARLOTTE
   (swallows her bite) I mean it this time.

                  AMELIA
    (cuts her pancakes) Say it anyway.

CHARLOTTE
(takes a breath) I think it's such bullshit when people say it's better to have loved and lost than never to have loved at all.

AMELIA
What do you mean?

CHARLOTTE
I just think it's so hypocritical. People wish they'd never been in love all the time. (looks down at the daisy next to Amelia's hand) Regretting things. Wanting to completely erase memories. People.

AMELIA
That's true. But what about the quote-unquote happiness you feel when you're in love. Does that just disappear when you've lost someone?

Charlotte picks up another daisy, twirls it once in her hand, then points it at Amelia.

CHARLOTTE
(smiles) I do believe in happiness, you know?

AMELIA
(plucks the daisy from Charlotte's hand)
I believe you. (nods twice)

CHARLOTTE
I'm not just miserable and judgemental all the time. (a beat) I'm happy when I'm with you. (places her chin in her hand then smiles)

Charlotte and Amelia stare at each other for a moment. Then they both break into laughter. Amelia turns away first. She looks down at her plate, takes a bite, then swallows.

> AMELIA
> So you'd rather forget.
> CHARLOTTE
> Forget what?

> AMELIA
> Forget that you were in love. Or forget the person you were in love with.

> CHARLOTTE
> Maybe not all Eternal Sunshine like that, but to an extent, I guess. If it's that painful, maybe it would be better to not remember. Or to not have done it in the first place.

> AMELIA
> You talk about love like it's something you do.

> CHARLOTTE
> It's an action. It's a choice.

> AMELIA
> It's a feeling. It's not in our control.

> CHARLOTTE
> I can choose who I fall in love with.

> AMELIA
> That goes against every romance book in the world.

> CHARLOTTE
> I chose to love you.

Charlotte looks down at the daisy in Amelia's hand. She takes it from her gently and brushes the petals with her thumb. She plucks one off and hands the daisy back to Amelia. She plays with the single petal in her right hand.

>AMELIA
>I couldn't help but love you.

Charlotte and Amelia stare at each other for a moment, then both look down and resume eating. They spend some time in silence. Enjoying each other's presence. A familiar song plays and Charlotte looks up at Amelia.

>AMELIA
>I love this song.

>CHARLOTTE
>I know.

Amelia smiles and returns to her plate. A few more moments pass. Charlotte takes a sip of her coffee.

>AMELIA
>Love is loss.

>CHARLOTTE
>Whatever do you mean?

>AMELIA
>I think when you love someone, you're accepting the possibility of being hurt. The possibility of losing them. And whatever pain that may follow.

CHARLOTTE
That's awfully selfless of people, isn't it? I think people are more selfish than that.

AMELIA
Maybe. But maybe not.

CHARLOTTE
How cryptic of you.

AMELIA
Do you accept the possibility of being hurt?

CHARLOTTE
By who?

AMELIA
Me.

CHARLOTTE
You'd never hurt me.

AMELIA
(laughs) Well not actually me. Losing me.

Charlotte swallows her bite then slowly looks up at Amelia.

CHARLOTTE
You're not dying, are you?

AMELIA
(laughs) No.

CHARLOTTE
Well, you can't leave me. I'd have no friends. No one likes me enough to get brunch with me every Sunday.

AMELIA
People love you.

CHARLOTTE
Not like you do.

AMELIA
(nods) Not like I do.

Charlotte and Amelia stare at each other for a moment. Amelia smiles then steals a bite of egg benedict from Charlotte's plate.

AMELIA
(chews and swallows) But would you visit my grave if I died?

CHARLOTTE
Never.

AMELIA
(gasps) You're a horrible friend.

CHARLOTTE
Maybe. But I think it'd hurt too much.

AMELIA
Okay. You're not that bad of a friend. (winks)

CHARLOTTE
(shakes her head and smiles, then sobers) I don't think I'd be able to wake up. Not to a world without you. Let alone go on about my day. Visit you, even.

AMELIA
But you can't sleep forever. And you'll need coffee. You love your black coffee.

CHARLOTTE
I do love my black coffee.

AMELIA
You should come here, as usual.

CHARLOTTE
Without you? Never.

AMELIA
But you say they have the best coffee.

CHARLOTTE
(takes a sip from her mug) They do.

AMELIA
So you have to come. I don't want you to give up your favorite spot.

CHARLOTTE
I'm not going to come alone. Every barista and waiter here knows us. They'll know something's wrong.

AMELIA
Who cares? I'd be dead.

CHARLOTTE
Don't say that.

AMELIA
Okay, fine. You should though. I'll put it in my will or something. Charlotte must keep coming to the café after Amelia's death.

CHARLOTTE
What did I just say?

AMELIA
That's the last time, I promise. (smiles)

Amelia picks up one of the three daisies remaining and plucks three petals off. Then she places the daisy next to the others on the table. Charlotte stares at Amelia's hands.

CHARLOTTE
I don't want you to haunt me.

AMELIA
I never said I would.

CHARLOTTE
I know you wouldn't. Not on purpose anyway. (a beat) You just would. I'd think of you all the time and see you in my dreams and just be reminded of you constantly. I just know it.

AMELIA
I'll try not to do that.

Charlotte laughs and picks up the second to last daisy from the cup, then points it at Amelia.

CHARLOTTE
And I'll try not to think about you.

AMELIA
(smiles) You can't blame me, can you? It really just sounds like a you problem.

CHARLOTTE
It really does, doesn't it?

Charlotte places the daisy on the table beside the other four sprigs and resumes eating. She glances up at Amelia every couple of moments. Amelia glances up too. Occasionally they make eye contact, and they both smile. The bell above the door rings and a customer walks into the café. Charlotte turns and glances at the door, then turns back to her seat. She sees her half-eaten egg benedict and mug of black coffee on the table in front of her, and five daisy sprigs laid out across the table with a few fallen petals around them. She looks up to find the seat across from her empty. No pancakes. No latte. No Amelia. She picks up the last daisy from the cup and twirls it between her fingers.

CHARLOTTE
(smiles and whispers) Happy birthday. I love you.

Emily Maddux

THE SIGNIFICANCE OF BEING STUPID

CHARACTERS

IRIS   College student in her early 20's.

REBECCA   Iris' roommate and friend, also a college student.

SETTING
An apartment in Wichita, Kansas.

TIME
Morning. Present day.

ACT I
SCENE 1
(A dirty apartment poorly furnished yet filled with books. Iris is lounging in a chair writing in her journal.)

IRIS

"I look down at myself and am surprised that my skin isn't transparent. I feel like a sound, yet one that wears away with each time I am heard, like an old piano sitting in an abandoned room. The notes soon become only memories."

(Rebecca enters)

REBECCA

What are you writing?

(Iris slams her journal closed)

IRIS

(annoyed) Nothing.

(Rebecca shrugs and sits down)

REBECCA

Okay. I just assumed that since we live together that you would be inclined to share your deepest darkest feelings with me.

IRIS

And I assumed that I would have an inch of privacy in my own home. (pointedly) Besides, I don't ask about what you do when you're alone. I'm surprised you ever are to be honest.

REBECCA

I hate my own company. What surprises me is how you don't.

IRIS

I believe that it was Oscar Wilde that said that to love oneself is the beginning of a lifelong romance.

REBECCA

There you go again.

IRIS

What?

REBECCA

Using other people's words because you can't think of your own.

IRIS

That's bullshit. It just sounds more poetic than the garbage that I can come up with. And just think? I've spent thousands of dollars on an education that taught me to recite dead white men. (pauses) Actually, don't think about it. It's depressing.

REBECCA

Good, I won't. (starts to stand) Hey, what do you say about getting out of this fire hazard of a used bookstore and get some food?

IRIS

No, I'm good. My brain is too muddled to worry about food.

REBECCA

(sits back down)

Anything I can help with?

IRIS

No, not really.

                             REBECCA

(defensively) Why because I'm too stupid to give good advice?

                               IRIS

That is not what I'm saying. (contemplates) Okay, you wanna hear it?

(Rebecca nods)

                               IRIS

(takes a deep breath) Recently, it has been proven to me that perhaps silence isn't wisdom, but simply stupidity. Last week I went home and visited my mom. There was a specific reason behind this visit, for I knew that my grandmother was in town with the intentions of spreading her husband's ashes.

                             REBECCA

Okay... So, you were upset that your grandfather passed away? (Iris stands and starts pacing the room)

                               IRIS

Bill never was my grandfather, at least, not on an emotional level. This is difficult to admit, but my grandma left my real grandfather in order to marry Bill because she was dissatisfied with her marriage. Bill lured her away from her family, knowing that she was married and that she was emotionally fragile. This was just the start for understanding Bill's character. For over ten years after, he would mentally abuse my mom right in front of my grandma, until she finally ran away and met my dad, searching for some sense of security. And what did my grandma do while this was happening? Absolutely nothing. Of course, I knew this before visiting, but it was my grandma's declaration that hit me the hardest.

REBECCA

(softly) What did she say?

IRIS

She looked me right in the face and stated that if she could go back in time, she would not have left my grandfather for Bill and that she regretted the over thirty years that she had spent with him. It was at that moment that I noticed how old and worn she looked, like a sandal that had spent a decade wasting away in the sun.

(Iris falls back into her chair)

Since then, I have been in an existential crisis.

REBECCA

And why is that?

(Iris looks around the room)

IRIS

I have read so many books, yet the words fly right past my eyes. What is the point of knowledge if one refuses to grasp it, like me? I could have said so many things to my grandma when she told me this, like how I was furious with her for subjecting my mother to Bill's abuse, all because she thought that she had to stick behind the poor decision that she made. She didn't understand that her life was as easy to change as a pair of clothes. She could have simply gotten up and walked right out the door! Yet I didn't say that. I could only nod as if because she was older, her decision was correct.

REBECCA

It makes sense why you didn't say anything. It would have been like kicking someone while they were down. You knew that it only would have added to the guilt that she was feeling.

IRIS

No, I didn't know that. I do this every time something real happens to me. I become silent. Whether it's discussing politics or being faced with any sort of adversity or...

REBECCA

Stop it. You are one of the smartest people I know. You were the one that told me that according to Socrates, true knowledge exists in knowing that you know nothing.

(Iris stands and resumes pacing)

IRIS

Well maybe Socrates was wrong! I know that I know nothing, but what good does that do!? All I do is ask questions and meet nothing but obscure answers that lead to more questions. And then when I am faced with an actual conflict, I either say nothing or spew some dead philosopher who might've been as confused as I am.

REBECCA

Hey, it's only ten in the morning. Can't this type of thinking wait until at least after noon? Look, you need to focus on a single thing that you believe to be true, and then continue with that. Like how I am going to need a drink after this conversation. That. Is. A. Fact.

IRIS

(sighs) See? You are so much smarter than me. You can look at life right in the face and see it for what it is. I on the other hand have to question every aspect of it, ending every fact with the question why or how. Because of that, you are bound to be content, and I am bound to live in the stupidness of my own creation.
(Rebecca contemplates)

REBECCA

Let me ask you something. Which is better? Asking too many questions or asking no questions at all? Or better yet, is foolishness the absence of knowledge or the non-acceptance of what has been already proven?

IRIS

(Iris sits)

What does it matter? I am both. A consistency of inconsistencies.

REBECCA

No this is important, so pay attention and stop looking depressing. Iris, you are only twenty-one years old. There is no need to expect yourself to know everything.

IRIS

Mozart was eight when he wrote his first symphony. Alexander the Great was eighteen when he conquered Greece. Pascal invented the flipping calculator at the ripe old age of nineteen. Your argument is stupid.

REBECCA

No. You not listening to me is. There are over seven trillion people on this earth. You and I are only two of those people. We are as inconsequential as sand. Wait, less than that, of atoms. Literally the conversation that we are having is going to fade away from our memories in less than twenty-four hours. That is the real reason why you don't speak when faced with a conflict and you know it.

IRIS

What?

REBECCA

You hold yourself up to such a high standard compared to these historical giants that anything that you deem to be less than, you throw away into the void that is your own mind.

(Iris goes still)

REBECCA

(softly) But do you wanna hear something else that I know? The people who love you do not care that you aren't Einstein or

Beethoven. They want to hear your thoughts, even if you are unsure of them. The everyday human being is supposed to grow in their beliefs. They're supposed to be a paradox of themselves. And sharing that process with others is how one comes to be remembered.

(Rebecca stands and picks up Iris' journal)

Your thoughts matter. This (waves the journal around) matters. As long as you know that, then you don't have to know anything else.

(a pause)

IRIS

But what about how to apologize for being a bad friend?

REBECCA

Oh, you haven't heard? There is a refresher course that is going to be taught at our favorite sushi place by yours truly in just a little bit, who is also going to conveniently forget her debit and credit cards at home.

(Rebecca helps Iris to stand)

She also should be the one to thank you. I realize that discussing your mom and grandma's pasts was difficult but know that I appreciate you telling me. That will surely not be forgotten.

IRIS
Thank you. I needed that wake-up call.

(They start to walk out of the room)

REBECCA

No need. We are all fools when it comes to being remembered.

Austin Schwartz

CHEKHOV

CHARACTERS IN ORDER OF APPEARANCE

ANTON CHEKHOV   A Russian physician,
                       author, and playwright

IVAN BUNIN   A Russian author,
                       a contemporary
                       to Chekhov

OLGA KNIPPER   Chekhov's wife

TOLSTOY
VOICE
STANISLAVSKI
PROFESSOR MICHAEL GOLDMAN
DIRECTOR
WILLIAMS
PEDESTRIAN

SETTING
The year is 1904. Chekhov's tuberculosis has reached its peak. It's currently the springtime and Ivan Bunin, a contemporary of novelist of Chekhov's, came to visit the Chekhov home to talk and visit with Chekhov before his health declines.

(The lights come up on a stage with CHEKHOV moving to sit down in a chair on the far left by a window. There is a bed on far stage right. CHEKHOV has a continuous slight cough throughout the scene, and it is only aggressive with the stage direction call for more coughing. BUNIN sets the "Cherry Orchard" down on the table center stage.)

IVAN BUNIN
So, this, "Cherry Orchard," you think it will be your last?

CHEKHOV
Why must we always talk about writing Ivan? Come sit with me and enjoy the view.

(CHEKHOV has a fit of coughing and then there is an awkward silence. BUNIN lifts up two drinks and brings them over by CHEKHOV before sitting down.)

BUNIN
Sort of ironic don't you think? To spend your last days at the "Orchard."

CHEKHOV
I've always enjoyed keeping trees, nurturing plants to grow. I used to feed the animals too when I could. I love life – to see it in action.

(CHEKHOV begins coughing once again.)

BUNIN
I hate to see yours fleeting so quickly.

CHEKHOV
I'll be fine. It's just a cold. Nothing to worry about.

BUNIN
Anton. You have fooled everyone long enough. A cold doesn't last for eighteen years, we all know that something is wrong but

you're too stubborn to say it. It's only gotten worse over time, especially over the past four. I don't mean to be insensitive, but you don't have long Anton. A few months, hopefully a couple more years – but you'll never make another decade.

CHEKHOV
Ivan you worry too much. My whole family does for that matter. I'm going to be fine. At the turn of the century, I was diagnosed with tuberculosis – nothing to fret to much about. It's Mycobacterium built up in my lungs.

BUNIN
That does not sound like nothing. You'd better figure out something to do about...

CHEKHOV
I'm the trained physician in the room and I'm telling you it's nothing to worry about.

BUNIN
You are out of practice.

CHEKHOV
I've told you medicine was always my passion. I enjoyed getting to interact with the common people. It gave me their perspective – I helped them live their life.

BUNIN
Yes, well that's never what provided support for your family. Nor is it where your greatest talents lay.

CHEKHOV
Writing is a mere hobby. Something that helps me cope and pass the time. Medicine is my lawful wife; literature is my mistress.

BUNIN
You need to recognize that you're good. Certainly, that piece that came from your trip to Yalta. What was it called?

CHEKHOV
"The Lady with the Dog."

BUNIN
A gorgeous love story that one was.

CHEKHOV
It's cynical.

BUNIN
It's poetic Anton. Stop selling yourself short. Your work is extraordinary. Your plays too.

CHEKHOV
They are laughable. Really just an examination of the average life of a Russkiye.

BUNIN
I want you stop being humble for one moment, please. The way that you construct these complex relationships in your stories is jaw dropping. It's so real!

CHEKHOV
That's because it is. I write what's real. I examine life and put it on a page. My mother always had a knack for storytelling. My talents came from my father, my soul came from Mama.

BUNIN
Wherever it came from you perfected it. There was that play you detested for some time. Your first I believe. It was named after a bird…

CHEKHOV
"The Seagull." The work was always impressive. It was the public that detested it, they couldn't understand the simplicity of life.

BUNIN
Stanislavsky changed that. If your name is on it, people want it.

CHEKHOV
This is the last one, it's the only one they commissioned and the only one they'll get. My writing is to be for my enjoyment.

BUNIN
Because in a way you are reliving your experiences.

(OLGA KNIPPER enters with letters in her hand. She comes through a door on the back of stage that to the audience would presumably lead deeper into the house.)

OLGA
I'm sorry to interrupt. You have more letters from your mother and sister. Masha actually sent two I believe. There is even one from your brother, Alexander.

CHEKHOV
Throw it away. You can bring the rest here.

OLGA
It's been years since you've heard from Alexander. I bet Masha told him you are getting worse. Siblings will always worry about one and other.

CHEKHOV
I'm not getting worse; I'm going to be fin…

(CHEKHOV begins to have another coughing fit.)

BUNIN
Maybe he has sent you his apologies for not visiting.

CHEKHOV
He has grown to be just as twisted as our father. Let me tell you it was despotism and lying that ruined our mother's youth. Despotism and lying so mutilated our childhood that it's sickening and frightening to think about it. I can even remember the horror and disgust we felt in those times when Father threw a tantrum at dinner over too much salt in the soup and called Mother a fool. Alexander is directly following Pavel's footsteps and I want nothing to do with it.

OLGA
Anton they are only worried about you and I am too. I was thinking we could travel when summer comes – once it's warmer out.

CHEKHOV
Olga, it's already April. It's warm enough to watch the trees blossom.

OLGA
I know. I've heard of a spa town in Germany called Badenweiler. It could be good for you to relax and stay in for different spa days. It might do you some good by speeding up your recovery. It wouldn't be too busy. It is in the Black Forrest so you will not feel overwhelmed by so many people.

BUNIN
Sounds like a good idea for you.

CHEKHOV
Alright dear we can go. We'll talk more about it later though.

(OLGA picks up their empty glasses and heads toward the door. CHEKHOV yells after her.)

We can try for early June.

(OLGA exits. CHEKHOV's attention is now returned to BUNIN.)

What were we saying?

BUNIN
That you must have taken inspiration from your life when creating your work. Your plays I mean. I know your short stories are a collection of people and events you have observed overtime.

CHEKHOV
I'd say that there has been moments or ideas I have because of something that happened in my life. But I've never written my experiences as if they were a fictional play. I only steal moments of my life because it's real. I tell real stories.

BUNIN
As an example?

CHEKHOV
The family in the "Cherry Orchard." They end up being bailed out of their financial crisis by Lopakhin, who in their situation destroys the family home's orchard. After my family had moved

to Moscow, I had remained in Taganrog, our childhood hometown, until I paid off the debts my father had neglected. A man by the name of Selivanov ended up bailing us out of our debt – the price for it being our family home.

BUNIN
I knew there must be something! May I take a guess at another?

CHEKHOV
By all means.

BUNIN
The relationship between Irina and Treplev is to replicate the one that you and Olga had when you were living in Yalta. She wanted to attempt being an actress in Moscow while you continue medicine, of course, but studied the Russkiye to further your writing career.

CHEKHOV
Yes. Although, there was not a competitive stepfather in my life that Olga fancied. I can say my dislike for my father played into Treplev's hate for Trigorin but that's to the extent it went. As well, you can see I have not shot myself.

BUNIN
I'm not entirely sure how I feel about that part of the piece. For all the comedic punches you put into the play it has a disturbingly dark ending. A lighter footnote may have been more appropriate.

CHEKHOV
My plays are comedies, but I don't write them to be funny – I write them to be real. Besides if I were to remove the gunshot then I would have to change the entirety of the play.

BUNIN
How so? It would just be the ending, which is simple as Treplev dies.

(CHEKHOV gestures to the stage around them when he explains this.)

CHEKHOV
I would have to terminate the rifle from the piece entirely and it would have become meaningless. When writing a play or even directing it - remove everything that has no relevance to the story. If you say in the first act that there is a rifle hanging on the wall, in the second or third act it absolutely must go off. If it's not going to be fired, it shouldn't be hanging there. This is even good advice for writing novels.

BUNIN
I guess that makes sense, if you are trying to maintain focus, but say you are just wanting to have an interaction with a huntsman during a story within the….

(Chekhov begins to have another coughing fit which grows to be worse than all the rest.)

Anton? Anton, can I do anything for you?

(OLGA enters.)

OLGA
Just bring him to his bed over here.

(OLGA and BUNIN help CHEKHOV over to his bed.)

He gets these bad one's sometimes. That's why I had a bed placed in the gathering room.

(OLGA and BUNIN lay CHEKHOV down on the bed. His coughing starts to go down slightly.)

BUNIN
I better get going. You'll need your rest if you are going to make that trip in a couple months.

CHEKHOV
I'm fine. I'm going to be fine. I've got plenty of time left, don't worry about me.

OLGA
Ivan is right. Just rest for a little while dear. I'll walk you to the door.

BUNIN
Thank you, ma'am.

(OLGA and BUNIN exit. CHEKHOV begins to cough again as the lights slowly close in on him. His coughing stops. After a pause.)

CHEKHOV
I'm going to be alright.

(The lights go down. 1904 - They come back up as a spotlight on OLGA side stage.)

OLGA
Anton enjoyed our trip to Germany. He wrote letters to his mom and sister of how well the recovery was going. I knew it was not. One night he sat up unusually straight and said loudly

and clearly, *Ich sterbe*—he knew almost no German. I learned that it meant, "I'm dying." The doctor calmed him, took a syringe, gave him an injection of camphor, and ordered champagne. Anton took a full glass, examined it, smiled at me and said: "It's a long time since I drank champagne." He drained it and lay quietly on his left side, and I just had time to run to him and lean across the bed and call to him, but he had stopped breathing and was sleeping as peacefully as a child...

(OLGA exits. 1906 - BUNIN AND TOLSTOY enter.)

TOLSTOY
Only seven years? I imagine that his writings will last longer than that. Did he say why only seven?

BUNIN
I was about to get to that Mr. Tolstoy. I asked him and he said, "More likely seven and a half. I've got six years to live."

TOLSTOY
I can assure it will be more than that. I've been a fan of his work for some time – I think I'll file his short stories into a collection to publish together. That should help get him at least seven more.

(BUNIN and TOLSTOY exit. 1915 - STANISLAVSKI enters.)

VOICE
For a look behind the play, please welcome Stanislavski!

STANISLAVSKI
"Chekhov often expressed his thought not in speeches but in pauses or between the lines or in replies consisting of a single word ... the characters often feel and think things not expressed in the lines they speak."

(STANISLAVSKI exits. PROFESSOR enters and begins to speak as if he is teaching a course. He appears to be from the 1940's.)

PROFESSOR (Michael Goldman)
Great question. Class - "having learned that Chekhov is comic ... Chekhov is comic in a very special, paradoxical way. His plays depend, as comedy does, on the vitality of the actors to make pleasurable what would otherwise be painfully awkward—inappropriate speeches, missed connections, *faux pas*, stumbles, childishness—but it's a part of a deeper pathos; the stumbles are not pratfalls but an energized, graceful dissolution of purpose."

(PROFESSOR exits. 1981 – WILLAIMS and DIRECTOR enter.)

DIRECTOR
"The Red Devil" was a masterpiece! You have to come back and write another one for next season Mr. Williams.

WILLIAMS
I've always desired to do a modern adaptation of Chekhov's, "The Seagull."

DIRECTOR
That sounds perfect to me!

WILLIAMS
I haven't even started.

DIRECTOR
You got yourself a deal old man. You're the best in our time and if you're using his work then I know nothing can go wrong with that duo.

(WILLIAMS and DIRECTOR exit. 2010 – PEDESTRIAN enters reading an article on their cell phone.)

PEDESTRIAN
"Of the many major European playwrights of the late 19th century, Anton Chekhov has lasted best of all. Of Chekhov's contemporaries, Shaw is in eclipse, Ibsen somewhat becalmed, Maeterlinck almost forgotten. Strindberg and Wilde still cut it in their different ways. None of them, though, connects as directly with such a large 21st-century public as Chekhov, born 150 years ago this month, still does. His short stories, his most important works, are revered. His four mature plays are rarely absent from the stage."
Wow. This guy must have felt like the all-star of his time. He had to have been a creative genius to make all his stuff up. Plus, I couldn't imagine what it must have been like to have no free time – he must have been writing every minute of the day.

(PEDESTRIAN exits. The lights come up on center stage where CHEKHOV is standing.)

CHEKHOV
"If you want to work on your art, work on your life. Do silly things. Foolishness is a great deal more vital and healthy than our straining and striving after a meaningful moment."

(Lights down.)

John Suffield

THE COMPANY

<u>CHARACTERS</u>

DEBRA — Just got laid off, gets confused and frustrated easily

CEO — A young person who is the CEO of The Company, she is very knowledgeable but can be very bratty at times

BARKEEP — A helpful barkeep with a French accent

DRUNK PEOPLE — (Two, male and female) Always drunk and passed out until "The Company" is said

(For the duration of this scene, the drunks will have their heads down until every time the phrase "THE COMPANY" is said, in which they will in unison lift their heads and cheer, yelling, "THE COMPANY!")

(The scene opens with the two people in the bar drunk, and the bartender cleaning the bar. DEBRA enters from stage left through the door.)

BARKEEP
He he he, ho ho ho (Frenchlike laughter), welcome to

the Good Bar! We're not great, we're not bad, we're good.

(DEBRA sits down at the bar looking quite sad)

BARKEEP
Hello madam, you can call me Barkeep, what might your name be?

DEBRA
Debra

BARKEEP
Oh well, it's nice to meet you, Deb, what can I…

DEBRA
It's Debra

BARKEEP
My apologies Debby, would you like a…

DEBRA
I told you it's Debra

BARKEEP
Ho ho ho (Frenchlike laughter) that reminds me of a funny story, I knew this woman by the name of Debrakinezor, but sadly we…

DEBRA
Are you deaf, I told you it's Debra!

BARKEEP
Debris? What do you mean debris? I don't see anything in the air.

DEBRA
I'll tell you one last time, and one time only… my name is DEBRA! And that is just Debra, nothing added, taken away, or substituted! You got that?

BARKEEP
Wait… you sure it's not short for Debracroploplis?

DEBRA
When has there ever been anyone with that name?

BARKEEP
I'll have you know that I have two cousins whose names are Debracroploplis, amazing women, both senators for New Jersey. Her husband is a doctor you know.

(DEBRA pauses for a moment)

DEBRA
Which one?

BARKEEP
Which what? Who are we talking about? Oh right! What can I get for you, Deb? A drink? A fresh meal?

DEBRA
I'll just have a beer for now, thank you.

(The BARKEEP hands DEBRA a bottle that has good beer written on it. DEBRA takes a sip.)

DEBRA
Wow! This is a good beer.

BARKEEP
I know! It's all good, not great, not bad, just good. So… what brings you to this fine establishment? No one comes to the good bar for a bad reason.

DEBRA
Well… Everything started the day I was born. I was born one morning when the sun didn't shine, I picked up my shovel and walked to the mine, I loaded 16 tons of number nine coal, and the straw boss said "Well bless my soul"…

BARKEEP
Isn't that just Sixteen Tons?

DEBRA
But that's not it, it gets worse. After work one day, chilling out, maxing, relaxing, all cool and all shooting some b-ball outside of the school. When a couple of guys who were up to no good started making trouble in my neighborhood, I got in one little fight and my mom got scared,
she said, "You're moving with your auntie and uncle in Bel-Air". Then…

BARKEEP
I'm pretty sure that that is the Fresh Prince of Bel-Air.

DEBRA
And that all brings me to the absolute worst part of my life, the final breaking point that leaves me in agony just thinking about it. This is the single event that left me spiraling out of control into the pit of despair that led me further into your bar this night…

BAREKKEP
Oh no! What in heaven's name could it be?

(Dramatic Pause...)

                DEBRA
           ... I got laid off.

              BARKEEP
Oh, I'm sorry madam. (Barkeep looks around and slowly sits down leaning into DEBRA.) You know... I've heard word around town the company is very desperate for workers if you're interested.

                DEBRA
      Oh really? What's it called?

              BARKEEP
What do you mean? I have already told you.

(A hooded figure, which is the CEO, walks in from stage left through the same door, and sits at the bar.)

                DEBRA
         No, you didn't.

              BARKEEP
          Yes, I did!

                DEBRA
No! You said the company was hiring!

              BARKEEP
           Exactly!

(An awkward silence of confusion occurs for a few short moments before it is interrupted by the CEO yelling)

CEO
Barkeep! Give me a glass of your finest… apple juice.

BARKEEP
Oh, right away Mrs. CEO!

(The barkeep hands the CEO a juice box.)

BARKEEP
Would you like anything, madam?

CEO
Get her the special, and put it on The Company tab.

(The BARKEEP goes behind the bar and brings DEBRA a water bottle)

BARKEEP
Here you go madam, our finest quality drink at the good bar, the special.

DEBRA
Thank you? What exactly makes it so special?

BARKEEP
Well… This drink is called the method because it gives a punch like Neil DeGrasse Tyson.

DEBRA
Don't you mean Mike Tyson, the famous boxer?

BARKEEP
Nope, this is scientific.

DEBRA
What?

BARKEEP
A scientific method. (BARKEEP gives a wink).

DEBRA
What does any of that have to do with the drink or punching? It's literally water, looks like water (smells the water) smells like water, (sips the water) and it even tastes like water, it's just plain water, there's not even a punch to it!

BARKEEP
Wow... that was a great hypothesis.
Oh! By the way, you know the company we were talking about earlier, this right here is our CEO!

(The CEO takes off her hood to reveal she is young)

DEBRA
Wow!

CEO
What?

DEBRA
You're the CEO? You're like 9?

CEO
I'm 12 and a half, thank you very much! I'm old enough to play the board game Risk since it's 10 and up, the trick is you put all your troops in Australia. My mom also lets me watch PG-13 movies... sometimes.

DEBRA
Oh really, oh look at the time, isn't it past your bedtime?

CEO
NO! (aside) My mom moved it to 10:30.

BARKEEP
CEO? She's looking for a job.

CEO
Oh! why didn't you just say earlier that you were a deadbeat? Come, let's sit at a table and talk business.
(DEBRA and the CEO sit at a table, and the CEO pulls out a rubber chicken or something like a chicken.)

CEO
Sell me this chicken.

DEBRA
Um… ok. (DEBRA picks up the chicken.) (Improvises a bad chicken pitch until interrupted by the CEO)

CEO
No, no no no no no no. Barkeep! Show em' how it's done.

(DEBRA hands the BARKEEP the chicken.)

BARKEEP
(To DEBRA) Are you hungry?

DEBRA
I could eat.

BARKEEP
Supply and demand my friend. (Throws chicken on the table.)

DEBRA
Wait… so what does (in finger quotations) The Company even do?

CEO
What do we do? Did she… did she really just ask what we do?

BARKEEP
I think she did.

CEO
You live under a rock? Everyone knows about The Company.

BARKEEP
We're a business for the sake of other businesses.

DEBRA
What businesses?

BARKEEP
That's our business!

CEO
and it could be yours?

DEBRA
What?

BARKEEP
To summarize…

CEO, BARKEEP, AND DRUNKS
We're the company.

DEBRA
So, you're that company?

BARKEEP
No, we're the company, that company is down the street next to their company

DEBRA
Who's company?

BARKEEP
No! they're on the other side of town next to our company. Although they used to be next to my company.

CEO
Oh yeah, I loved my company, they were the nicest people.

BARKEEP
They really were, I remember when…

DEBRA
Alright! I've had enough of this madness! You all are crazy! I'm leaving!

(DEBRA begins to leave but is stopped in her tracks by the BARKEEP)

BARKEEP
Hold on. At least have a good meal before you leave. I'll make it a good one.

DEBRA
Fine! But I'll only have one steak and then I'll leave.

(The BARKEEP goes behind the bar and pulls out a platter with the stake on it and brings it to her.)

DEBRA
What's this?

BARKEEP
You said you wanted a steak.

DEBRA
Yes, I want beef.

BARKEEP
But we do not have beef, we have only just met and I hold no ill will towards you.

DEBRA
No! Cow! Cow!

BARKEEP
(Gasp) how dare you! I am no cow, that is very rude of you to say! You know? I think now, we do have beef!

DEBRA
If you have beef then get me my steak!

BARKEEP
I already did!

DEBRA
That's a stick! Why don't I throw it and you fetch it, you DOG!

CEO
Alright, let's settle down now. Listen, I don't think you fully understand how we do things here at the company. Here, pitch me an original idea.

DEBRA
I don't know

BARKEEP
Come on, it's not that hard, anything that comes to your mind.

(DEBRA shrugs still not having an original idea.)

CEO
Alright, I'll give you an example. First, you take a person and you combine them with a fish, and BOOM! Original idea. I'm telling you, no one has ever thought of this before. Apple, Microsoft, even Disney.

DEBRA
You mean a mermaid…

CEO
NO! THAT'S MY ORIGINAL IDEA! YOU CAN'T STEAL IT! I'LL SUE YOU!

DEBRA
Ok ok, hypothetically, if I join the company RIGHT NOW, THIS IS JUST A JOB. IF I ADVANCE ANY HIGHER IN THIS COMPANY, THIS WOULD BE MY CAREER. AND, UH, IF THIS WERE MY CAREER, I'D HAVE TO THROW MYSELF IN FRONT OF A TRAIN.

CEO
Nope, wouldn't work.

DEBRA
And why is that?

CEO
We own the trains.

DEBRA
Are you serious?

CEO
As serious as a dead man.

DEBRA
What?

CEO
(sigh) I'm dead serious!

DEBRA
Alright, you know what? I don't have anything to lose. I accept your offer and I'll start immediately if it will only get you to be quiet.

CEO
Really? You really meant it? You'll really join The Company?

DEBRA
YES! How much will I be getting paid?

CEO
Barkeep, how much do I pay you?

BARKEEP
I make 14… a year… sometimes Tuesdays?

(DEBRA is visibly very confused when an alarm goes off and the drunks get up.)

DRUNK 1
Alright sweetie, that's enough playing for one day.

CEO
But it was just getting fun.

DRUNK 2
I know, but you know the rules, at 10:30 it's time for bed.

CEO
But mooom… daaaaaad?

DRUNK 1 AND 2
NOW!

(The parents leave stage left and the CEO follows. The CEO stops before she leaves and turns to DEBRA.)

CEO
Thanks for playing with me, my name is Friendella, but my friends just call me Friend.

(DEBRA being visibly confused turns to the BARKEEP.)

DEBRA
I think I'm going to need another good beer

BARKEEP
(without a French accent) Sorry, playtime's over so it's time to go home, goodnight.

(BARKEEP exits stage left)

(All that is left on stage is DEBRA looking very confused.)

(Black out)

The Jeanne Lobmeyer Cárdenas Prize in Short Fiction & The Sr. Madeleine Kisner Prize in Poetry

The Jeanne Lobmeyer Cárdenas Prize in Short Fiction and the Sr. Madeleine Kisner Prize in Poetry is awarded each year. Journal staff members handle preliminary judging, and all submissions accepted for publication are considered. Winners are then selected by distinguished, nationally-recognized writers. Past judges have included Michael Arnzen, Doris Betts, Bruce Bond, Scott Cairns, Marta Ferguson, Lise Goett, Albert Goldbarth, Jeanine Hathaway, Laura Kopchick, David Lunde, Paul Mariani, P. Andrew Miller, Christopher Moore, Virginia Stem Owens, Timothy Richardson, Barbara Rodman, Vicky Lee Santiesteban, Philip Schneider, Tim Seibles, Richard Spilman, Sonya Taaffe, Jeanne Murray Walker, Albert Wendland, Ned Balbo, Douglas Ford, and Marge Simon.

Jeanne Lobmeyer Cárdenas

Jeanne Lobmeyer Cárdenas, Professor Emeritus at Newman University, received her Bachelor's degree from Sacred Heart College (now Newman University) and her Master's degree from Marquette University. An award-winning press writer, Professor Cárdenas taught literature, writing, and journalism at Newman, imparting her passion for language to students. The Jeanne Lobmeyer Cárdenas Prize in Short Fiction continues Professor Cárdenas' influence on the careers of student writers.

Sister Madeleine Kisner

Sr. Madeleine Kisner, A.S.C., held a Bachelor's degree from Sacred Heart College (Newman University), a Master's degree from Creighton, and a Doctor of Art from the University of Michigan. A published poet and writer, Sr. Madeleine taught her students both the music and the craft of words during her twenty-year teaching career at Newman. Sadly, Sr. Madeleine has passed, but the Kisner Prize in Poetry continues her work with future generations of poets.

2023 FINALISTS

Poetry

i saw icarus die today	Tatyana Hill
love letter from an earthworm	Sofia Jarski
The Shape I Take	Elise LeMonnier
To Cast a Shadow	Anna McElhannon
Divine Mirth	Samuel Schmidt
When I lift the Weight Off My Shoulder	Kayla Shields
Autumn's Gift	Hope Strickbine
Sacristan	Hadassah Umbarger

Prose

Inbox	Zoey Birdsong
What He Wants	Ila Kumar
The Face of Death	Kaylee Patterson
Ill-Fated	Rachel Patterson

Prose Judge—Sharon Emmerichs

Sharon Emmerichs was born in Sweden to American parents and grew up in Wisconsin near Lake Michigan. She has been a writer all her life, from the time she scribbled 'words' and pictures on pieces of paper, stapled them together, and called it a book. Her love of stories later translated into an English degree, and then she went on to get her MA and PhD in medieval and early modern literature… and because she collects degrees the way some people collect stamps or baseball cards, she graduated with her creative writing MFA in fiction in 2021. She is an Associate Professor of Shakespeare and medieval literature in beautiful Alaska, where she lives with Juneau, the derpiest Siberian husky ever.

Poetry Judge—Bryan Thao Worra

Bryan Thao Worra is an award-winning Lao poet from Minnesota. The author of ten collections and over 100 publications around the world, he has presented at the London Summer Games, the Smithsonian, the Library of Congress, the Singapore Writers Festival and over 60 colleges, museums, libraries and special events focusing on the power of the imagination to change lives. He holds over 20 awards for his writing and community leadership and served twice as the president of the international Science Fiction and Fantasy Poetry Association.

A NOTE

This is the last issue of *Coelacanth*, at least for the foreseeable future. There were extenuating circumstances, and for now, this is where we stop.

But we only stop publishing a collection. We only stop publishing a celebration. We only step back from the boundaries of this journal format, and from the tradition of college students reading their peers' work and compiling it. We do not stop pursuing literature. We do not stop celebrating prose and poetry and all the gray spaces in between. We do not stop recognizing that there is something good, true, and beautiful about desiring to create art and share it with others. This avenue for doing that is leaving. We will find others.

Artists are stubborn creatures, kind of like weeds, and the absence of a formal platform does not mean that we will stop being artists.

If you were wanting to contribute to *Coelacanth* in the future, I encourage you to submit to another journal. This is not the only one out there! But I even more strongly encourage you to allow yourself to be the kind of person who accidentally writes poems walking through their dining room, and who can't sleep because they're thinking about the character arc they need to fix in their latest short story or novel seed, and who stops in the middle of their walk across campus to take a picture of the way the sun is hitting the trees.

We are only stopping putting words inside a book with a dead fish on the cover. It's up to you to continue to find ways to live your life with the words and art that spills out of you. You are charged not to stifle it, and not deny it existence.

It's a noble charge. Will you accept it?

Hadassah Umbarger
Editor-in-Chief, 2023

Made in the USA
Columbia, SC
25 September 2024